AN ISLAND APART

Lillian Beckwith was born in Ellesmere Port, Cheshire, where her father owned a grocery business, thus providing the background for her book *About My Father's Business*.

Shortly before the war she went to live in the Hebrides, where she stayed for nearly twenty years, living and working on her own croft. Her experience there resulted in her Hebridean books.

Her hobbies are cooking and entertaining, beachcombing and travelling.

AN ISLAND APART

Lillian Beckwith

ARROW

Arrow Books Limited
20 Vauxhall Bridge Road, London SW1V 2SA

An imprint of Random House UK Ltd

London Melbourne Sydney Auckland
Johannesburg and agencies throughout
the world

First published in 1992 by Century

Arrow edition 1993

1 3 5 7 9 10 8 6 4 2

Printed and bound in Great Britain by
Cox & Wyman Ltd, Reading, Berkshire

ISBN 0 09 914031 4

For Geoff and Grace, with love

Glossary

Ciamar a Tha? How are you?
Slainthe Mhath! Good health!
Mho ghaoil. My dear.
Oidhche Mhath! Good night!
He Fooar. It is cold.
Ceilidh. A meeting for gossip and song.
a chiali mo chridhe. My dearest dear.
Bheinn. Wife.

The light from the street lamps was veiled by a heavy, wind-harried drizzle intermixed with sleety warnings of impending snow. The city pavements were slushy beneath the feet of jaded shoppers and homegoing workers who, with shoulders hunched, chins muffled into scarves and with faces crumpled into scowls of resentment against the weather, scurried to catch transport to their destinations before the increasing wind should urge the snow to launch a full attack.

Amidst the crowds two figures, a man and a woman, could be singled out in sharp relief. They neither hurried nor jostled but paced composedly side by side; their shoulders were not hunched; their faces were not crumpled into scowls but rather lifted unconcernedly to face the drizzle. They neither conversed nor exchanged a perceptible glance and though they were plainly together their attitude was one of separateness, as if it were obligatory they should keep a prearranged distance between them so creating the impression that they were as indifferent to each other as they appeared to be to the harshness of the weather.

The stocky figure of the man looked cosily enough clad in a thick homespun jacket which gave the appearance of being only bedewed by the drizzle as did his deerstalker hat pulled well down over his forehead. His ungloved hands seemed to hover tentatively in the region of his jacket pockets as if resisting their offered protection; his sturdy laced boots trod the pavement with the confident gait of the born countryman.

The woman, slightly shorter and only a little less stocky than the man, carried a tightly furled umbrella under her arm despite the fact that her macintosh had draped itself

1

in a browbeaten way around her figure as if signalling that it was no longer able to repel the unremitting drizzle. Her black cloche hat had tightened and shrunk away from the auburn hair which patently it had been designed to confine; her lisle stockings, liberally splashed with pavement slush clung wetly to the calves of her legs while the limpness of her worn brogues betrayed the fact that they had not adequately protected her feet.

Evidently not seeking any kind of transport the couple walked on, leaving the clang and bustle of the city streets for the less hurried and more muted noise of the suburbs. Skirting the entrance to a gloomy park with its attendant stone cold statues they crossed a short thoroughfare where a cinema, a fish and chip shop and a public house were showing signs of stirring themselves to welcome the evening's patrons while at the same time most of the daytime traders were douting their lights and closing their shop doors to discourage further custom.

Beyond the thoroughfare the road ended almost abruptly in a quiet avenue lined on either side by tall trees whose winter-bare branches only partly screened long terraces of substantial houses, once the homes of well-to-do citizens but long since converted into boarding houses and flats, small private schools and offices. As the couple were about to turn into the avenue the man slowed his pace and touching the woman's sleeve, murmured interrogatively.

She paused only to give a nod of assent and immediately he retraced his steps in the direction from which they had come. The woman carried on but as if the small diversion had brought to her attention the fact that the rain had eased off and the houses gave more shelter from the wind she carefully unfurled her umbrella, raised it above her head and continued along the avenue.

When she reached the entrance to a house which bore the name *ISLAY* in gold lettering on the dimly-lit fanlight she mounted the six stone steps and producing a key from her pocket, inserted it into the door lock and entered the vestibule where she took off her soaked macintosh and

2

her hat and hung them on one of the stout wooden hooks. She did not take off her gloves. Shaking her umbrella gently – it was not very wet – she looked dubiously at the umbrella stand as if debating with herself whether or not she should leave it there. The umbrella was recently acquired and a very special gift and she intended to take good care of it. She was not going to let Isabel even set eyes on it if she could help it, she told herself. Isabel had no compunction about borrowing anything she fancied nor about the state of the thing if and when she returned it.

Deciding to take the umbrella up to her room she opened the door into the hallway to be assailed, as she had expected to be by the appetising smell of steak and kidney pudding. She experienced a surge of relief. Everything appeared to be in order. Not, she reminded herself, that there was much that could go wrong with a well-prepared steak and kidney pudding. Though rightly her half day off-duty should have started at two o'clock she had stayed on not only to prepare the pudding but also to bake a plum tart in readiness for the evening meal and because she reckoned that the best steak and kidney puddings needed slow gentle cooking she had set the pan to simmer before she had gone out, reassuring herself that short of an unlikely gas failure there was virtually nothing anyone could do to ruin it. Not even Isabel, she reflected, her mouth tightening grimly at the thought.

She was about to climb the stairs up to her room when she was hailed by a shout from the kitchen. 'Is that you, Kirsty?'

'It is myself,' she responded.

A door at the far end of the passage was flung open to reveal a glimpse of a clean but dowdy kitchen from which the tempting smell was wafting more deliciously into the hallway. A tall angular woman stood in the doorway wiping her hands on a towel. 'Thank the Lord you're back. I was praying the rain would drive you back early so you'd be in time to help me,' the woman greeted Kirsty fretfully before turning to re-enter the kitchen.

Kirsty rested her umbrella against the bannister hoping Isabel was too distraught to have noticed it and followed her into the kitchen where Mac, Isabel's husband was slouched in an armchair, his face covered by a newspaper, his stockinged feet splayed out as if to deliberately trip the unwary.

'Is anything wrong, Isabel?' Kirsty asked with only a pretence of surprise. In her experience nothing ever seemed to go right for Isabel.

'Wrong? Just about everything's gone wrong,' wailed Isabel. 'For a start I booked in three extra guests only an hour or two ago. A couple and their son and now that wretched Meggy hasn't turned up. I tell you I'm in such a bourac I don't know which way to turn next.'

'Why would you be in a bourac? The meal must be almost ready and after that's cleared away you have only to pop the hot water bottles into the beds and take the guests their evening tea and biscuits and then the evening will be free,' Kirsty reproved her mildly. She was accustomed to Isabel's imagined bouracs.

'Didn't I tell you there'll be three extra mouths to feed?' Isabel demanded.

'I don't see that as being a worry,' retorted Kirsty. 'There's plenty of steak and kidney pudding and also plenty of plum tart to fill three extra mouths without anyone having to go short. You know I always err on the generous side.'

'Too much,' sniffed Isabel. 'But the point I'm making is that there are no potatoes peeled nor carrots either.'

'That's only to be expected. It is Meggy's job to see to the vegetables when she comes,' Kirsty told her calmly.

'But she hasn't come in,' Isabel snapped.

Kirsty darted a quick glance at the kitchen clock. 'She's certainly late,' she allowed. 'But supposing she doesn't turn up at all there is still plenty of time for you to peel

4

the potatoes and prepare the carrots ready for the evening meal,' she soothed.

Isabel confronted her, hands on hips and eyes lit with anger. 'Me? Peel potatoes when you're here to do it. If Meggy's not here then it's your job.'

'No, not on my half day off,' Kirsty corrected. 'And really, Isabel, you can't pretend you have all that much to do even without Meggy,' she reasoned.

'You can just forget about your half day off and see to those vegetables,' Isabel ordered irascibly. Turning quickly she tripped over her husband's feet and stumbled against the corner of the dresser. Kirsty did not move. 'Don't just stand there like a log of wood,' Isabel berated her as she rubbed at her arm. 'Just go and get changed and put on an overall. You're not paid to watch me work.'

Kirsty's chin rose fractionally. 'And you can mend your manners,' she told Isabel in a tight voice. 'I am not used to being spoken to in such a way and you will please not speak to me ever again like that.'

'Really?' taunted Isabel. 'I'll decide how you'll be spoken to, not you. D'you hear that, Mac?' she mocked, snatching away the newspaper that covered her husband's face. 'Milady here is telling me I mustn't speak to her as if she's just a servant. She really does believe she owns the place now.' Mac grunted a startled expletive.

Kirsty took a few seconds to compose herself before she countered, 'I will give up my time off to help you but only because I care about the comfort of the guests. I will not be ordered by you to do so. I may be only a paid servant as you choose to call me but if you ever speak to me in such a way again I will pack my belongings and walk out of that front door and, guests or no guests, you will not see me again.' She paused, aghast at her own recklessness while Isabel, startled by the sudden outburst, could only retaliate with an incredulous glare.

'I will go now and change into dry clothes and then, by my own choice, I will come down to the kitchen,' Kirsty continued resolutely. 'There need be no panic about the evening meal being ready on time. I will see to that because I care about the comfort of the guests and I will help clear away afterwards but then I shall take the rest of the evening off as is my due.'

'Oh, thank you for nothing,' Isabel attempted to sneer, and as Kirsty was closing the kitchen door behind her she heard Mac's voice asking scornfully, 'Where in Hell does the old boiler think she could go if she walked out of here, I'd like to know?'

Lazy, good-for-nothing lout, Kirsty reflected angrily as she climbed the stairs. Since he's at home why doesn't she get him to prepare the vegetables?

Once in her room she hastily took off her damp clothes, changed into dry stockings and slipped on a pair of house shoes. Finally she put on a plain black dress. The dress was by no means a stipulated uniform, ISLAY not meriting such a degree of formality but apart from the suitability and economy of plain black she liked to wear it in the evenings considering it complemented her smooth pale skin and enhanced the rich auburn of her hair. She was not, nor ever had been, vain about her appearance and now at nearly forty years of age and with a sturdy rather than a shapely figure, she had accepted that she could aspire only to be neat and clean in her person and dress.

Shaking out her abundant hair which, she knew, was the only feature that preserved her from plainness, she towelled it dry before pinning it into a loose bun. That done, she surveyed herself in the wardrobe mirror, glanced at her bare hands, and satisfied with her appearance was tempted momentarily to further aggravate Isabel by dawdling before she went down to the kitchen. But pride in her own standards and in upholding ISLAY's reputation quickly banished the temptation and since there now seemed only a slender chance of Meggy turning up in time to serve the evening meal she decided it would be wiser to do it herself rather than risk the sulky Isabel upsetting the guests by her inattention.

She was halfway down the stairs when the doorbell

rang. 'I'll answer it,' she called in the direction of the kitchen, being sure she knew who would be waiting to enter.

'Ah, 'tis yourself, Mr MacDonald!' she greeted the man as she opened the door. 'Come away in now out of the rain.' Though hardly more than half an hour had elapsed since they had parted company her tone had the same easy cordiality with which she greeted all *ISLAY* guests.

Mr MacDonald seemed a little nonplussed by the impersonality of her manner. He swallowed nervously before he spoke.

'Indeed I will be well pleased to do that,' he acknowledged in an undertone as he stamped his boots on the thick doormat.

Once inside the vestibule he produced from his jacket pocket a half bottle of whisky which, a little diffidently he offered to her. With a gesture of dismissal she pushed his hand back towards his pocket and ushered him into the hallway. 'Go you now and get into a dry jacket and I will hang this one in the kitchen where it will dry overnight,' she instructed. He looked a little dashed and a tiny patch of redness appeared high on his cheekbones. Kirsty treated him to an explanatory nod of her head in the direction of the kitchen. Instantly nodding his comprehension he slipped the half bottle back into the jacket pocket.

'Just you get yourself into some dry clothes,' Kirsty repeated, her voice taking on a louder note as they entered the hallway. 'You could easy catch your death.' Acknowledging her advice with a hesitant smile and more vigorous nodding he began to climb the stairs. She watched him covertly, disguising her interest by a show of rearranging a vase of artificial flowers on the chiffonier. Not until she heard the door of his room close did she go into the kitchen.

'You've taken your time,' Isabel grumbled. Kirsty ignored the allegation. Moving away from the sink Isabel dried her hands on the roller towel and took a packet of cigarettes from her apron pocket. 'My God! What an afternoon!' she complained, collapsing into a chair and immediately lighting a cigarette. 'Talk about rush. I've never had to rush so much in all my life.'

'Meggy hasn't come then?' Kirsty asked, starting to peel the potatoes.

'No!'

'Has there been any word from her to say why?'

'Nothing. Not a squeak from the little bitch,' Isabel snapped.

'I hope she's not ill or that she's not met with an accident,' Kirsty observed anxiously. 'It's not like Meggy to let folks down without a word.'

'She's very likely been put off by the weather,' Isabel said tartly.

'I'd say that was most unlikely,' Kirsty contradicted. 'She's always been very punctual and weather has never put her off before.'

'Maybe she's found herself a boy friend at last,' Isabel sneered. 'With a squint like hers she'd be that glad to get a fellow to take some notice of her she'd very likely forget all about having a job to go to. She'll get her notice when she does turn up unless she's got a good excuse, I'm telling you.'

'She's always been a jolly good little worker and I'm sure there's an excellent reason for her not coming,' Kirsty insisted.

'Anyway, with no Meggy to serve the meal you'll have to attend on the guests or else tell them to help themselves or go hungry. I've set the tables but I'll not wait on.' She tossed her head, plainly confident of Kirsty's compliance.

'I will do all that is necessary for the comfort of the guests,' Kirsty stressed. Isabel flicked her a smug glance and left the kitchen.

The meal was served at the regular time and when the tables had been cleared and the guests had gone about their various evening activities Kirsty washed and dried and stacked away the dishes. She was standing by the stove filling a thermos flask with hot tea ready to take up to her room when the door opened and Isabel and Mac entered the kitchen bringing with them the mingled smell of scent and cigarette smoke. Seeing that they were both dressed in their outdoor clothes she glanced at them with raised eyebrows and waited for them to speak.

'We're away to the flicks,' Mac announced in a slurred voice which betrayed he had already taken a substantial evening dram.

Kirsty made no comment.

'You'll have to see to the ten o'clock tea and biscuits for the guests and pop the hot water bottles into their beds,' instructed Isabel, pulling on her gloves and looping a scarf around her neck.

Kirsty fought to control her rising indignation. Putting down the flask she turned to face them. 'Indeed I shall do nothing of the kind,' she asserted. 'Must I remind you that it is still my half day off and tonight as I have already told you I particularly wish to have the time to myself.'

For a second or two she was able to rejoice at their flabbergasted expressions before she went on, 'When your aunt was in charge here I was never called upon to work during my time off unless there was a special reason for me to do so and then, more than willingly, I gave up my time.'

'She was a damn sight too soft with you!' Mac interjected testily.

Ignoring him Kirsty looked straight at Isabel. 'You will not be trying to tell me that going to the cinema is any kind of a special reason?' She screwed the cup firmly on to the flask.

'But you'll be here in the house, won't you? It's surely not much to ask you to do us the favour of taking in tea and biscuits and seeing to the hot water bottles. It won't take you more than a few minutes,' expostulated Isabel.

'No, it is maybe not much to ask,' Kirsty agreed. 'But you did not ask me, did you? You told me I would have to do it.' She reached for a cup and saucer, took a couple

9

of her own baked scones from a tin and set them on the tray with the flask.

'Just you stop this hoity toity,' Mac interposed more as if he felt it was time he contributed in some way to the disagreement rather than in the hope of ending it.

With a gesture Isabel silenced him. 'It's the last night of a film we particularly want to see and if we stay to the end it'll be too late to see to the guests. They'll have gone to their beds.' Her manner was only a little less unpleasant.

'What d'you do on your nights off anyway? Just sit in your room knitting or reading stuffy old books or listening to the wireless?' jeered Mac.

'Just that,' affirmed Kirsty equably. 'And that is exactly what I am planning to do this evening.'

'You'd still have time to do all that,' Isabel quibbled. 'You wouldn't have to forsake your pleasure for more than a few minutes to oblige us.'

'That's true,' Kirsty acknowledged. 'But tonight I am not intending to oblige you. As you can see I have my own supper here on the tray which in a moment or two I shall be taking up to my room and then I shall not be coming down to the kitchen again until the morning.' She surveyed them coolly. 'You must learn that I am not a slave to be hectored and bullied as you two have tried to hector and bully me. You must get back from your cinema in time to attend to the guests or,' she continued, 'you can tell them they must get their own tea and biscuits and see to their own hot water bottles tonight.' Again Kirsty was surprised at her own audacity.

For a full moment the couple glared at her without speaking as if convinced that their glares were menacing enough to weaken her resolve. Disregarding them she picked up her tray and with a curt 'goodnight' started towards the door. Seemingly dumbfounded by her unexpected outburst the couple moved sullenly to let her past.

'See that!' Isabel remarked spitefully as Kirsty opened the door. 'Wouldn't think of doing anything for anyone but herself.' Mac opened his mouth ready to speak but Isabel went on, 'You'll just have to stay here or go to the cinema on your own.'

'What the . . . ?' Mac began to protest but before he could continue Isabel cut in. 'Go on, I wouldn't be able to enjoy going out now. Not after all this nastiness.'

Seemingly unperturbed Kirsty carried her tray to the stairway. She could still hear the couple wrangling in the kitchen. 'Well, haven't I told you often enough. It's your own fault. Never mind what you promised your aunt. Give the bloody woman her notice. You can manage without her,' Mac rebuked his wife.

'Oh, shut your mouth and go,' Isabel snarled at him. With a muttered oath he came shambling past Kirsty and jerking open the vestibule door let it slam behind him.

Up in her room Kirsty switched on the light and drew the curtains. The wind-swept sleet scratching against the window reminded her of the cold outside and, lighting the gasfire, she drew her chair as near as she dared to its hissing warmth. She sat stiffly, giving her clenched nerves a chance to relax, for despite her show of composure during the altercation with Isabel and Mac, she had felt outraged at the way they had spoken to her. Now in the privacy of her room outrage waned slowly into self-reproach for having been stupid enough to allow such a shabby pair to crack her customary forbearance. Tonight, especially tonight, she had needed to be calm so as to ponder over the events of the past few days.

The dispute had not been her fault, she comforted herself. It wasn't her nature to be easily roused to angry retort. A child of the Hebrides, she had been inculcated since birth with the pride and the tolerance of the Islander: with the essentiality of masking anger with placidity. She was no stranger to censure. There had been trying times even when her friend Mrs Ross had been the owner of ISLAY, for though the old lady had always taken great pains to ensure that guests were respectable and well-behaved, there had been the inevitable misfits and bracing herself to endure their crankiness had imbued in Kirsty an equanimity of character that had proved well able to withstand provocation.

The unpleasantness in the kitchen had not been her fault, her mind reiterated and yet the conviction tended to rebound interrogatively. It had begun trivially enough so could it have been her own too hasty reaction that had resulted in it developing into such a peevish wrangle?

She could so easily have yielded and agreed to give the

guests their late tea and biscuits, and it would have been very little trouble to her to put hot water bottles into the beds and thus enable the couple to go and see their wretched film. But she had acquiesced so often when they had made demands on her free time that they had become arrogant even to the point of giving the impression that she should be beholden to them for allowing her the freedom of choice!

The desolating knowledge that she could not continue at ISLAY had settled in her mind – but so had the realisation that at her age it might not be easy to find a position that would suit her. She had come to accept that she would have to endure the situation at ISLAY as long as she possibly could . . . until today. Today her life had suffered a sea change!

Settling more comfortably into her chair and taking up her knitting, she let her mind travel back to the well-remembered day nearly twenty-five years previously when, as a naive fourteen year old, she had stood timidly on the front door-step of ISLAY clutching in her hand an envelope addressed to 'Mrs Ross of ISLAY' in which was a letter signed by the Reverend Donald MacLean, minister of the Church of Scotland, testifying that Kirsty had been born and brought up on the Island of Killegray by her Granny Morag MacLennan. It had gone on to state that he had known Morag MacLennan personally during his time there and that she was a good widow-woman and a good churchgoer. Her death four years earlier had resulted in Kirsty being sent to an elderly aunt, also a good churchgoer, who had resided in his present parish in the city. A year ago, he'd explained, the aunt's health had deteriorated and she had gone to live in a Home, and since Kirsty had no other living relatives he and his wife had felt they ought to be responsible for her. His wife had seen to it that the girl was well-trained and she would vouch for her good character.

Kirsty had been shown the letter before it had been put into the envelope and had nodded diffident approval.

13

She'd noticed that the minister had made no reference to her parents. She hadn't been surprised. No one had mentioned either of her parents in her presence since the day she'd asked her Granny, 'Where is my mother?' She'd expected to be told gravely that her mother had 'passed on', but instead her Granny had cackled light-heartedly, 'Ach, she took one look at you and straightway took herself off to Canada or some such place.'

Kirsty had tried to be similarly light-hearted. 'And my father?' she'd pursued. 'Ach, didn't your mother get you from some fellow in Glasgow. I doubt she'd know more of him than you do yourself. He's best put out of mind.'

Kirsty had been too unused to affection to be much disturbed that neither of her parents had wanted her. Such accidents were not rare in the Islands and the 'cailleach', as she'd always called her Granny, had brought her up and in an offhand way, had bestowed on her a degree of affection that had saved her from feeling rejected.

She'd been nervous as she'd reached up to press the bell at the side of *ISLAY*'s front door and even more so when the door was opened by a short, plump, white-haired lady with blue probing eyes behind gold-rimmed spectacles.

'You will be Kirsty MacLennan, will you not?' the lady had asked.

Kirsty had held out the letter. 'I am to give this to Mrs Ross,' she'd managed to say.

'I am Mrs Ross and you see the name *ISLAY* above the door so give me the letter and come away inside so I can take a good look at you,' the lady had said, leading Kirsty into the kitchen at the back of the house.

All Mrs MacDonald, the minister's wife, had told Kirsty was that Mrs Ross was looking for a servant girl to help her run her boarding house and had asked a friend if she knew of anyone who might be suitable. The friend had told Mrs MacDonald and so Kirsty's name had been put forward. Mrs Ross was reputed to be a shrewd but tolerant woman who demanded good and reliable service from her employees. Her previous servant had been with her for fifteen years before she'd left to get married, the minister's wife had emphasized.

As Mrs Ross had scanned the letter the minister had written Kirsty had hoped she would not ask her about her parents. City people, she had discovered, were mighty curious about such things but Mrs Ross appeared to be satisfied with the minister's recommendation. After scrutinising Kirsty for a moment or two she'd said, 'D'you think you'd like to come and work for me?' Kirsty had nodded seriously. 'You would?' Again Kirsty had nodded. 'Have you not got a voice, Kirsty MacLennan? You'll need one if you're going to work for me.'

Kirsty had seen that the blue eyes were lit with teasing. 'Yes, please,' she'd replied eagerly.

'And have you got a good sense of humour – for that's something else you'll feel the need of here.'

Kirsty had smiled back at her. 'I believe I might have,' she'd said demurely.

Mrs Ross had agreed to take her on a month's trial and, if she proved suitable, to train her as a cook-general. Grateful for the offer and relieved at the prospect of getting away from the repressive atmosphere of the Manse, Kirsty had set out to please her employer in every way she could and as a result, had been at *ISLAY* ever since. Under Mrs Ross's tuition she had soon become an excellent cook and in time had matured into a reliable and willing helpmate, even being trusted to look after *ISLAY* herself when her employer's presence was required elsewhere. The relationship between herself and Mrs Ross had soon developed into warm companionship despite the difference in age, and under their joint supervision *ISLAY* had prospered. Kirsty had come to regard the guest-house as her much-loved home and was as proud of its sound reputation as was her employer. The hours she worked were often demanding; her wages were relatively meagre but never at any time had she questioned her good fortune in having such congenial employment.

Thus, for her, the years had passed as contentedly as she would have wished and since Mrs Ross had always staunchly maintained that she would continue to run ISLAY 'Until the Good Lord sees fit to take me' – and in the same breath would assure Kirsty that when that day came she would not want for a home, Kirsty had come to regard her position there as more or less a sinecure. Even bearing in mind that Mrs Ross was a good deal older than herself and that the signs of her increasing age were beginning to manifest themselves, Kirsty had reckoned that her own stamina and experience would ensure the continuation of ISLAY with scant need for Mrs Ross's presence, save as a kind of benign overseer. But there were years of life left in the old lady yet, she had told herself, and had deferred considering any other future for herself.

There had been no hint of change even eighteen months previously, when Mrs Ross had returned after attending her brother-in-law's funeral. Because the old lady had disapproved of her sister's second husband she had never before visited their home neither, to Kirsty's knowledge, had she ever expressed an interest in doing so. Now, however, she was keen to describe to Kirsty its comforts and conveniences. 'Such a lovely little resort, quiet and a rare view of the sea,' she had enthused. 'And no stairs to climb, Kirsty and no dust you'd notice even after a week. And there's a garden full of flowers and shrubs and space enough to put out a table and a couple of chairs if you've a mind for taking a cup of tea outside.'

Kirsty had listened with a suitable degree of interest. 'You'll maybe be wanting to take a wee holiday there when we're not busy,' she'd suggested.

'Indeed, isn't that just what my sister was telling me I should do,' Mrs Ross had admitted. 'Irene and I kind of lost touch with each other when her first husband died. He was a nice enough laddie but when she took up with this other fellow I had no time for him. I wouldn't have thought of going to see my sister while he was alive, but I daresay things could be different now.'

Kirsty allowed herself an enigmatic smile, recalling that on the rare occasions sister Irene and her undisciplined child Isabel had visited *ISLAY* Mrs Ross had found it as hard to conceal her displeasure at their behaviour as she had had to conceal her relief at their departure. Nevertheless, Kirsty had encouraged her employer to spend a holiday at her sister's home. Harmony between relatives was desirable, she believed, and anyway a couple of weeks quietness and seaside air might do the old lady a power of good. She and Meggy, the new young servant, could cope well enough on their own.

Mrs Ross had enjoyed her holiday and, as Kirsty had hoped, had returned much invigorated by her spell away from the clamour of the city. The blow had come three months later after Mrs Ross had again visited her sister, but this time she had been absent only a few days. On her return she had been noticeably perturbed and Kirsty, suspecting that perhaps the relationship between the sisters had once more become a little less cordial, had diplomatically limited her enquiries to the restorative effect of the visit. Her questions seemed to make the old lady evasive and Kirsty had begun to wonder if there had been a serious disagreement between the sisters. It had not been until two days after her return that Mrs Ross had enlightened Kirsty as to the cause of her evasiveness. They had been sitting in the kitchen, polishing the brassware, when Mrs Ross had admitted that she had been getting very tired of late and it had been worrying her enough to see the doctor. He'd told her she'd got high blood pressure and needed to take things easier.

In a distraught voice she'd continued, 'It's going to be a terrible shock to you, Kirsty, and a terrible wrench for me to give up *ISLAY* but worst of all is going to be losing your companionship. You've been such a good friend to me since the day you first set foot here.'

Dabbing at her eyes she'd become aware of Kirsty's stunned expression and reaching across the table to squeeze Kirsty's hand she'd gone on, 'Oh, I wish you could come with me but there isn't enough room in the bungalow. I've thought and thought about it all, wishing we could both be together, but you know well enough that I'm old and much as I've always wished it I know now I shan't be able to carry on at *ISLAY* even with you at my side to help me.'

Kirsty could only stare at her speechlessly. 'Not that we shan't be able to see each other often,' the old lady had gone on to assure her fervently. 'There's a good train service between here and my sister's place so you'd be able to come and see me on your day off, and I shall surely be coming to see how things are at *ISLAY* whenever I can. We'll not lose touch.'

'You mean you are leaving *ISLAY*?' Kirsty had managed to echo faintly.

'Yes, my dear.' Mrs Ross stifled a sob. 'I couldn't say a word before it was all settled in case you'd worry yourself sick, but what's been arranged is for my sister's daughter, that's my niece, Isabel, you remember Isabel, don't you? A right naughty little madam she was when she was young, but of course she's grown up now and has got herself married, and she and her man have been thinking of looking for a guest-house so Isabel will have something to occupy her while Mac, her husband, is out at work.' Mrs Ross's mouth twitched derisively. 'I don't reckon on Mac being up to much but it's Isabel who'll be running the place so that's no matter. You'll be here to see she does things right and,' her voice became earnest, 'it's such a comfort to me to know that *ISLAY* is going to stay in the family so to speak.' She squeezed Kirsty's limp hand. 'And you'll never want for a home, my dear, that's a condition of the lease,' she'd assured her, a note of triumph in her tone. 'Mind you, I don't believe I would have had to make it a condition. Isabel knows fine how lucky she is that you'll be here to help run the place and see it keeps up its good reputation. After all, she's had no experience other than being an usherette in a cinema.'

Kirsty was appalled. Her mind seemed to have gone

numb; her tongue had dried in her mouth and she had been unable to speak. Mrs Ross had looked at her anxiously. 'You will stay and help, won't you, Kirsty?' she'd asked and had immediately answered her own question. 'Surely you will – ISLAY's your home almost as much as it's been mine.' Her tone became pleading. 'I never doubted you'd want to stay on here. What would ISLAY be without you?'

Kirsty had tried not to show her despair. She'd managed to say in a choked voice, 'I don't suppose I shall have much in the way of an alternative.'

'But surely you've always been happy here at ISLAY, haven't you, Kirsty? Haven't we both agreed that it's been grand the way the two of us have worked together all these years and never a cross word between us? I want for nothing more than that you should continue to be happy here.'

Kirsty had at last managed to clear her throat. 'I've always been very happy here at ISLAY with you, you must know that well enough.' This time it was she who had reached out to squeeze her employer's hand. The touch let slip their emotions and for a few minutes there was a sobbing silence.

When Kirsty had regained control of her voice she'd said, 'You ask what ISLAY will be without me, but ISLAY without you can never be the same again. You have been to me what I would have wanted a mother to be. I cannot see myself ever being happy here again.'

'I pray to God that you will be,' the old lady had murmured. 'And I just want you to believe that your position here will be safe as ISLAY itself,' she'd continued feelingly. 'You need have no fear about that. Even though she's my niece I've insisted the solicitor puts it into the lease. Isabel has to agree that you must be allowed to stay here on exactly the same terms as you've always been used to from me, for as long as you yourself wish to. The choice will be yours but I hope to God for ISLAY's sake you'll choose to stay.' And there the matter had rested.

After Mrs Ross had departed to live with her sister, Isabel and Mac had immediately installed themselves as the new proprietors of *ISLAY*. It had taken a very short time for Kirsty to discover that, unlike her easy-going aunt, Isabel was a captious, ill-tempered and penny-pinching woman who not only lacked the experience but hadn't the temperament to run a highly regarded guest-house such as *ISLAY* successfully. As for her husband, Mac, Kirsty relegated him to the lower class of boorish lout.

It had seemed to her extraordinary that Mrs Ross had allowed herself to be deluded into believing such a couple could be considered suitable to take over the running of the establishment which she herself had built up by hard work, and in which she had such pride, but there was no gainsaying that she evidently had been so deluded. How much had Isabel fawned on her aunt to obtain her consent to such an arrangement, Kirsty wondered. She was never to know. Six weeks after her retirement Mrs Ross had suffered a severe stroke which seemed to have virtually wiped out her memory and deprived her of the power of speech. Kirsty could only shrug her shoulders and reconcile herself to the sadness of change.

Throughout the months following their occupancy Kirsty had carried on trying as subtly as she could to counteract the many changes Isabel was keen to introduce but soon the evidence of *ISLAY*'s deteriorating reputation as a good class guest-house was all too plain. Enquiries and bookings became steadily scarcer while complaints from guests became more frequent.

Kirsty had to face the wretchedness of knowing that her own position there was unlikely to be as secure as she had hitherto envisaged it to be. Not for a moment had she let herself believe that Isabel would be foolish enough to imagine she could cope without her, at least for some time anyway but her own need to steel herself to overlook the changed atmosphere – the penny-pinching on food, Isabel's archly dismissive manner to guests who dared to voice their complaints, her overbearing treatment of

Meggy – and not least, her supercilious attitude towards Kirsty herself had alerted her to the limitations of her own endurance. Secretly she'd begun to cast around for other employment, but she was already thirty-nine years old and apart from being a good plain cook she had few other skills to offer in a city where women nearing forty were regarded as being of use only for scrubbing floors or for the scrap heap. Oh well, if the worst came to the worst she could always scrub floors, she'd had to comfort herself. Until today . . .

Not until she'd heard the clatter of the trolley being pushed into the Smoking Room had Kirsty risen from her chair and poured herself a cup of tea from her flask. Taking a scone from the tray she again settled into her chair, and as she slowly sipped and nibbled her anger dispersed, her grim expression softened and a smile began to curve her lips. The smile spread until she was capturing her bottom lip between her teeth and pressing the palms of her hands against her cheeks in an effort to suppress the laughter that was threatening to convulse her.

When she had her laughter under control she lay back weakly in her chair, her eyes tear-bright, her head moving dazedly from side to side as if stunned by her own thoughts. Dear God, but today she'd done it! She might have acted rashly but she'd done it, hadn't she? Yes, she convinced herself, she'd done something which only last week she wouldn't have conceived it possible that she'd even consider doing. And she was GLAD! The word seemed to shout itself into her mind nearly triggering off another burst of laughter. There would never again be a degrading scene such as that she had endured in the kitchen this evening. After today she had an effective rejoinder for Isabel and Mac. She had been strongly tempted to use it as soon as Isabel had shown signs of irascibility this evening but consideration for the guests had prevailed. Tomorrow was time enough, and then it would be the sort of rejoinder they deserved.

The gasfire popped its warning that it needed sustenance. Guiltily she fed it a couple of pennies. She was averse to wasting pennies on gas but she knew that this evening it would take some time before she could compose herself to face her bed and sleep. Her thoughts were still swirling around the momentous happenings of the past few days, and she willed herself to pin her mind on the precise moment she believed it had all begun. The moment, ten days previously, when in response to the ringing of the doorbell she had opened the front door of *ISLAY* to admit the person whose name was recorded in the book labelled Expected Arrivals as Mr Ruari MacDonald, West Isle – due Friday p.m.

On that day there had been a fierce wind and incessant rain.

'You will be Ruari MacDonald, I'm thinking?' she enquired of the man who stood on the doorstep. He answered her question with only a cursory salute. 'Then come away inside now, do,' she welcomed him with her customary civility, urging him into the vestibule while she hastily closed the outer door against the wind-whipped debris of late autumn leaves which were intent on soiling the clean tiled floor.

'It is a cruel wind, is it not?' she continued, 'and more rain this one day than would disgrace a week.' As she chattered on she appraised him swiftly, noting that he neither wore nor carried a waterproof. She'd gained the impression that he was totally untroubled by the weather and had immediately surmised he belonged to the Highlands or Islands where, she was only too well aware, wild weather was too constant to be much heeded.

In the vestibule he stood uneasily awaiting her further instructions, a stocky country-looking man of average height and, she'd judged, of middle age, clad in a thick homespun suit and cap. His only luggage was a stout canvas bag. Even after the door was firmly closed he was slow to move from the mat on which he was standing and, sensing his shyness, she held out a welcoming hand.

'I'm Kirsty MacLennan,' she introduced herself. 'I'm sort of head cook and bottle-washer here as folks say,' she explained with a friendly grin.

Eagerly he grasped her proffered hand and shook it vigorously.

'Kirsty MacLennan,' he acknowledged in a voice that was barely more than a whisper and then with growing confidence he repeated, 'Mistress Kirsty MacLennan, is it?' as if he wished to fix her name in his memory.

'Oh, everyone calls me Kirsty, just,' she told him. His manner relaxed and a relieved smile settled on his face. 'Through here, if you please,' she invited him, pushing open the door into the hallway. 'Now, Mr MacDonald, if you will write your name in the book there just,' she indicated the register lying open on the chiffonier. 'Then I will show you your room, or maybe,' she paused for a moment before going on to suggest, 'Maybe you would sooner leave your luggage down here and go straightway into the room we know as the Smoking Room overby where there's a good warm fire that will take the chill off you.'

She hadn't liked to suggest he might dry his clothes there in case he thought she was referring to his lack of a waterproof. 'There's none of the other guests back yet so you'd have the room to yourself. The meal isn't served until six-thirty but if you've a mind for it I can easily bring you in a pot of tea and a scone to put you on till then.'

He received her suggestion with a muttered 'Aye, aye,' that had sounded pleased enough, but he'd made no move. My, my, but he's awful shy, she remembered thinking to herself. She indicated the register more pointedly and then he stepped forward. Taking a snowy-white handkerchief from his pocket he carefully wiped both hands before picking up the pen that stood in the inkpot but as he bent forward, a couple of drops of rain fell from the peak of his cap on to the page. She heard the slight catch of breath and noticed his oblique glance at her, almost as if he expected her to reprimand him for not having removed his cap. With a dismissive smile she stepped forward and blotted the page.

'There now,' she approved. 'Now, will I take your cap and hang it in the vestibule where it can drip to its heart's content?' she offered.

He took it off carefully and handed it to her. When she

24

returned from the vestibule she said, 'Now?' and looked at him enquiringly, gesturing first towards the stairs and then in the direction of the Smoking Room. He seemed so hesitant that it had crossed her mind that this could be his very first visit to the city. She felt a surge of compassion for him.

'Perhaps I should show you to your room then,' she decided for him, and led him up the stairs. 'See and come down into the Smoking Room when you're ready just, and I'll bring you some tea,' she instructed him.

'Aye, indeed, I will be pleased to do that,' he assured her and added coyly, 'Folks mostly call me Ruari, if you've a mind.' She nodded understandingly.

In the kitchen while she was occupied with the preparations for the evening meal her thoughts strayed from time to time to ponder on the reason for Ruari MacDonald's visit to the city and, more pressingly, the reason why he had chosen to stay at ISLAY? To her knowledge, on the rare occasions when Island folk undertook a journey they were generally most careful to ensure that accommodation would be provided or arranged or at least recommended by relatives or connections of relatives, no matter how remote, where they could be certain of being in contact with other Islanders who spoke their language and, in Island parlance, 'would not make a stranger of him.'

Had Ruari MacDonald been naive enough to assume that because a guest-house bore the name ISLAY it would, without doubt, be owned or managed by someone with strong connections with the Island of that name? If so, he would be quickly disillusioned. The truth was that ISLAY had been the name of the house when Mrs Ross had taken it over, and since she had seen no point in going to the expense of having the gold lettering on the fanlight removed, she had simply carried on using the same name. As for the probability of meeting other Gaelic speakers, he might just as well have chosen to stay at a boarding house called SHAN-GRI-LAH, which was the last house in the block, or even SAMARKAND which was situated in an adjoining avenue. Mrs Ross herself had no knowledge of the Gaelic language and indeed had never met an Islander until the day Kirsty had presented herself at the front door.

Was Ruari MacDonald perhaps pursuing some secret mission of his own and deliberately avoiding meeting anyone who might detect his secret, Kirsty asked herself. That, she thought, would be a typical way an Island man would go about it. Perhaps *ISLAY* was just a stop on what was to be a long journey. To Canada, perhaps or America or Australia? She shrugged, scolding herself for her curiosity. Ruari MacDonald's presence was no concern of hers anyway and she would be wiser to simply slot him into the register of undistinguished guests who comprised *ISLAY*'s usual clientele.

When she heard the door of the Smoking Room open and then click shut she took in the promised tray of tea and scones. Ruari MacDonald was standing by the window when she entered. She noticed that he'd changed into a dry jacket and had slung the wet one over the guard in front of the blazing fire. Immediately she became aware of the mingled smells of bog myrtle and peat reek emanating from the steaming jacket; smells that evoked the moorlands of her Island childhood and although she had never fancied returning to the island where she had been born and bred, she experienced a few seconds' waft of nostalgia as she was setting down the tray.

'Indeed it's a day to be hiding oneself from the weather,' she observed.

'It is indeed!' he echoed. 'It is not a good day at all.' He turned round to face her but had not moved from the window. 'You have no liking for the rain?' he ventured to ask.

'I have no liking for city rain,' she told him. 'And I would say neither will you yourself when you've seen more of it.'

'Ach, but I'm used to far worse rain than I've seen today,' he confessed.

'I have no doubt you are used to heavy rain in the Islands,' she countered, 'but compared to the stuff the sky throws down at us here which soils everything it touches, Island rain is as clean and fresh as a baby's tears.'

He took a confident step towards her, his eyebrows raised in pleased surprise. 'You know the Islands?'

'Well enough,' she admitted. 'Was I not born on an island and was I not brought up there by my Granny until I was near ten years of age?'

He stared at her with undisguised delight, the shyness ebbing away from his smile. 'Wasn't I after thinking you had a kind of sound and look of the Islands about you,' he'd responded promptly. There was a momentary pause before he probed coaxingly, 'Then you would have the Gaelic, surely?'

'I once had the Gaelic right enough,' she corrected him, 'but since I've neither heard nor spoken a word of it for over twenty years it's myself would be surprised if I still have more than the bare bones of it nowadays.'

Eagerly he offered her a Gaelic greeting and when, with barely a moment's hesitation she returned it, his eyes shone with keen pleasure and he continued addressing her in the language which in her childhood had been her native tongue. The effect on her was as startling as if she had been given a welcome though unexpected caress but he spoke too fluently, catching her offguard, and she wasn't sure she perfectly understood what he was saying. Too sensitive to risk making a fool of herself by giving an inept reply she thought it safer to acknowledge his attempt to converse with her with no more than a regretful shake of her head accompanied by a rueful smile.

'My memory of it has gone from me,' she admitted.

He was anxious to test her further but the ringing of the doorbell demanded her attention and with a pout of feigned disappointment she escaped from the room. Afterwards she managed to convince herself that she was glad of the interruption, yet at the same time she was conscious of a sense of mixed shame and regret that she found it difficult to recall her native language. All evening the brief exchange with Ruari MacDonald persisted in her mind and when she retired to her bedroom that night she set herself to recall how much she still retained of her native tongue, testing her memory and surprising herself by the degree of her recall. Why, she needed only to practise it, she decided, and it would soon come back. She began to hum softly the tunes she'd learned at the winter ceilidhs and with the tunes came the words and with the words came the images of the singers and of the old crofts where the ceilidhs mostly took place. The notion came to her then to enquire if there was a Gaelic Society near enough for her to attend their meetings so as to renew her acquaintance with the language and with the Islands from which she had allowed the city to wean her.

During the days that followed she and Ruari MacDonald had little contact, meeting and greeting each other casually only in the dining room when she was helping to serve meals or to clear away the tables. However on the eighth day following his arrival she was collecting the morning mail from the post box on the front door, ready to sort it and place it in the racks for the guests when she noticed that one of the envelopes bore no stamp. Wondering why the postman had not rung the doorbell to demand the appropriate fee she examined the envelope more keenly. With some surprise she saw that it was addressed to 'Miss Kirsty MacLennan, ISLAY'. That was all; no avenue, no street and no town. Since she herself rarely received letters she spent a few moments conjecturing whether it was really meant for her and just who the sender might be. It must be for her, she decided. There was no one of that name at ISLAY except herself, nor had there been anyone named MacLennan for the past six weeks or more and he had been no 'Miss'. Concluding that it was probably from a neighbour who was working for some charity and wished to enlist her help for some function she slid the envelope into the pocket of her apron with the intention of opening it when there were fewer demands on her time.

It was not until after the mid-day meal when she had the kitchen to herself, Isabel having gone off to a whist-drive, Mac to a billiard hall and Meggy not yet due to report for her spell of evening duty, that Kirsty had time to sit down and make herself a pot of tea. Taking the envelope from her pocket she again scrutinised the hand-writing, seeking some clue as to the sender but she had no success. Probably a hired helper, she guessed, and reached into the table drawer for a knife to slit open the envelope. It contained a single sheet of ruled paper and immediately she began to read the wording she was thankful she was sitting down.

'*Dear Kirsty MacLennan*', it began. '*After our little chat the evening I arrived I am wishing to tell you I am of a mind to take a wife and I'm after thinking you could suit me very well. If you have such a mind also that way you will maybe leave a message in my room where no one else will see it so we will maybe arrange a time to speak over the matter. Your friend, Ruari MacDonald.*

P. S. I must tell you I am to be away back to my home by Wednesday first so as to be there ready for the cattle sale.'

Feeling completely winded by the shock of receiving such a letter, she read it six or seven times before she was able to allow herself to grasp that it contained a proposal of marriage. The first proposal she'd received in her thirty-eight years! As comprehension focussed itself in her mind she had a desire to laugh wildly. 'The Dear!' she ejaculated under her breath. 'The Dear, Dear!' she repeated. She poured herself another cup of tea and her hand was so unsteady she slopped some into the saucer. Hastily she substituted a clean saucer before picking up the letter and reading it yet again, her head shaking with incredulity. What nonsense indeed! What sort of joke was this to play on her? But if it was nonsense her mind could not detach itself from musing, lightly, over his proposal. The revelation that she now knew the reason Ruari MacDonald had come alone to the city and why he had chosen to install himself at *ISLAY* rather than an establishment frequented by his kinsmen startled but did not wholly surprise her. He had come with the intention of seeking a wife and he'd wanted to lose no time about it! It was not unthinkable. She'd heard her Granny say there was occasionally a shortage of marriageable women on some of the more remote islands and that men would sometimes 'suffer painfully from yearnings'. She'd thought then that 'yearnings' was a stomach ulcer or rheumatism, which seemed to be a prevalent illness in the Islands, but whatever had prompted Ruari MacDonald's desire to seek a wife, Kirsty realised it was a very daring thing for him to have done. And certainly it had been wise of him to try to conceal his intention from his kinsmen. Young as she'd been at the time she could even now recall the merciless teasing a bachelor neighbour had endured when there'd been a rumour that he was so anxious to seek a wife he had gone to the length of putting an advertisement in a newspaper. How would shy Ruari MacDonald have reacted to similar waggery? she wondered.

But she was still of the opinion that to have chosen herself as a possible wife was nonsense. Whatever could have put it into the head of such a timid, gentle man that she would make a suitable wife for him? A woman he hadn't set eyes on until a week previously. A woman he'd barely exchanged more than a few words with. It was almost improper to think of such a thing. Just nonsense her thoughts reiterated, and persisted in reiterating throughout that day and the whole of the following day and, careful as she was to avoid exchanging even surreptitious glances with him when she was in attendance in the dining room, the scornful phrase continued to assert itself.

And yet, because of the changed circumstances at *ISLAY* she urged herself to consider his proposal, no matter how ludicrous it at first seemed and as she considered it she was conscious of a small tingle of excitement which she was reluctant to recognise. She remembered Mrs Ross asking her one day if she'd ever been tempted to get married or, more bluntly, if she'd ever had a fancy for being penetrated by a man?

When Kirsty had indignantly denied any such temptations the old lady had complimented her. 'You're a wise lass, Kirsty. See and stay that way. The more a man has his way with a woman the sooner he'll tire of her.' She'd tried then to coax Mrs Ross into telling her of her own experience of marriage but the old lady had brushed off her curiosity with cynical abruptness. She wished now that it was possible to acquaint Mrs Ross with Ruari MacDonald's proposal but, alas, the old lady was past clear-headed conversation. There was no one else she could or would have wanted to turn to.

Mentally Kirsty allowed herself to list Ruari MacDonald's virtues. He was an Islesman and for that reason alone she was prepared to trust him. Island men were shrewd. His decision to offer her marriage would not have been made without keen observation and after deep reflection. He struck her as being quiet and clean. He gave every indication of being considerate, kind and intelligent. Even Meggy had spoken of his thoughtfulness. Would it be unwise of her to encourage him by agreeing to discuss the possibility of becoming his wife? There would be so much she would need to ask him and doubtless there was much he would want to know about her. She reviewed her own qualifications. She was a good cook and a competent housekeeper. She was strong; she was penny-wise yet not frugal. She reckoned she wouldn't be the sort of wife an Island man would be ashamed of.

After forty-eight hours wrestling with her misgivings she decided she would agree to his suggestion that they should meet and discuss the subject of marriage. She would slip into his bedroom the following evening while the guests were in the dining room and put a note on his dressing table telling him she could be certain of having the kitchen to herself the next evening once the meal was over. Isabel and Mac were invariably out until after midnight on Monday evenings and he would be welcome to come and take a 'strupak' with her. She thought her use of the word 'strupak' would serve to put him at ease although she herself hadn't heard or used the word for 'a cup of tea and a chat' since she had left her Island home after her Granny had died, but she'd never forgotten the cosiness of the image it brought to mind.

The following evening, a few cautious minutes after the front door had closed behind Isabel and Mac, Kirsty heard footsteps approaching the kitchen. To spare him, for she was certain it was him, the embarrassment of knocking and possibly risking being observed by another guest she rose from her chair and opened the door before he reached the threshold.

'*Ciamera a Tha!*' he greeted her. There was a bashful grin on his flushed face and a smell of whisky on his breath, not strong but evidently he'd felt the need to stiffen his courage before confronting her. Detecting it made her feel obscurely reassured.

'*Ciamera a Tha!*' she responded, smilingly indicating a chair she'd already placed between the stove and the table and opposite her own, but before he sat down he produced an unopened half bottle of whisky from his pocket and with eyebrows raised enquiringly held it for her approval.

She nodded perfunctorily. As a child she'd once been coaxed into taking a 'wee dram' at New Year 'to condition her' as had been explained. She'd hated the smell, the taste and the effect it had had on her and even after she'd reached adulthood, save for a rare medicinal hot dram when she'd been suffering from a heavy cold, she'd taken whisky only on each New Year's eve when Mrs Ross, whose regular Saturday night 'tassie' it had been, had prevailed upon her to share a celebratory drink. But she'd known instinctively that Ruari MacDonald would take it as a rebuff if she were to refuse the drink he offered.

Compliantly she took two glasses from the cupboard above the sink and set them, along with a jug of water on the table and while he opened the bottle and poured the whisky she busied herself making a pot of tea and putting out a plate of scones she'd baked that afternoon.

'*Slainthe Mhath!*' he declared, raising his glass with a flourish and taking a mansize gulp.

She, too, raised her glass. '*Slainthe Mhath!*' she echoed, taking only a sip from her glass before nodding with the simulated approval she knew to be necessary.

The toast lessened the initial constraint between them but even so they continued to talk banalities, each too imbued with the Island reticence to approach a subject until it had been prefaced by a suitable exchange of irrelevant conversation – and then only obliquely. Touching first on his impressions of the city they drifted effortlessly to speaking of the circumstances which had led to her being there. She was frank about her unidentifiable father; about her mother's desertion; about being brought up by her Granny – the 'Cailleach' as she'd called her; about Uncle Donny who was Granny's only son and who had always stayed at home because he'd been considered too 'far back' to go to school.

For some reason she herself could not be sure of, she had been guarded about speaking of Uncle Donny since she had come to the city. Even to old Mrs Ross. City folk didn't understand such small strangenesses in a person, she'd decided, aware that even at home in the village Uncle Donny had been mockingly known as 'The Dummy' because he could only produce a sort of 'whoop' at the back of his throat when he'd tried to communicate with anyone but, sensing her listener's readiness to comprehend, she shed her restraint and chattered about him easily. Uncle Donny hadn't been lacking in sense, she defended him to Ruari. And he'd been big and strong though he could be awkward and clumsy at times. But he could be tender and gentle, sometimes crying over a sick animal and never would he wring the neck of a wee hen even if such an important person as the missionary was likely to be in the village and expecting to be offered a meal. There was no doubt Granny could never have managed to work the croft without him doing the heavy work, she stressed, and his only misdoing so far as she could recollect was taking himself off to the hills without giving anyone a sign that he was going and then staying there for hours at a time, not even coming back to take his potatoes and herring though many were the scoldings he'd got from Granny about it. But more often than not when he did come back he'd bring some plant or flower that she and Granny had never before seen but of course he hadn't been able to tell them where he'd found it unless they'd been prepared to go with him and be shown the place.

When Granny had died folks said poor Donny couldn't be left to look after himself so he'd been sent to a Home, a fate which Kirsty obviously regarded as being far worse than being sent to an elderly relative as she herself had been. A minister had occasionally brought her scant news of him from which she'd deduced he had been very unhappy at the Home. It appeared that though he'd been kept clean and well-fed the Home had been too grimly supervised. He'd fretted because there were no animals for him to look after and no hills or moors for him to wander. The grounds surrounding the Home had been enclosed by iron railings rather than the rough dykes he'd been accustomed to scrambling over and the only visible greenness had been well-disciplined hedges and lawns which had been mown so rigorously he'd been feared to tread on them.

She'd managed to get messages to him via the minister telling him she hoped to visit him 'soon enough' but since Donny had never been able to write she'd had to glean from the minister small tit-bits of information about his well-being. She'd always nursed a hope, she confided to Ruari, that when she was older she'd maybe have a home of her own where she'd be able to have Donny and look after him but she'd been less than two years in the city when the minister had called to tell her that Donny was very poorly indeed. She'd not had a chance to see him before he'd died. She blinked away her tears.

'My own mother had such a one in her own family,' her companion commiserated. 'It is true they need a lot of understanding.' She glanced at him gratefully, realising that she felt suddenly uplifted as if speaking of Donny after so many years had erased a sense of guilt that had lain dormant since his death.

For a few moments they stayed silent and then she again was burrowing deep among her earliest memories and tossing them to him for comparison. They soon became engrossed in sharing recollections of their child-hood, each plucking at scenes that remained embalmed in their memories. They talked of the hard work of the croft, recalling with pride how young they were when they carried home their first creel of peats; their first pails of water from the well; of how secretly pleased they were to be trusted to help to dig potatoes; to bind and stook the newly-cut corn; to rake and build prapachan of freshly scythed hay.

They contrasted their memories of schooldays and the idiosyncrasies of their teachers; they chuckled over their recollections of Halloween mischief; gloated over the sea-sonal pleasures of collecting gull's eggs; of fishing with home-made rods and lines for the small brown trout that hid in the quiet pools by-passed by the rushing burns, or for sea fish from huge rocks that jutted out from the shore. She recalled the ecstasy of splashing about in the peaty brown water of the lochans after a hot, windless day's work or play.

'Hamish, the post, taught some of us to swim,' she told him. 'And I was well pleased about that when I came to the city because I could go to the swimming baths with the scholars. I soon learned to dive too,' she added.

He looked impressed. 'I never did such a thing,' he said regretfully. 'There was no one to teach us at the school and the lochans on our island are so deep and thick with reeds, we were forbidden to try.' He considered a moment. 'Maybe we should have gone in the sea more but there were so many jobs to be done at week-ends and on holidays that when the weather was calm we didn't get much time. I suppose that was the way of it.'

'I daresay it would be so,' she agreed.

'I'm thinking maybe you liked the city when you first came to it?' he asked.

She thought she could detect a trace of wistfulness in his tone. 'I liked my first taste of it well enough,' she admitted. 'It was exciting. The trams and the shops and the streets all lit up and full of people. The church bells ringing on Sundays and livening up people before they went to church. My! I was that taken with it all. And I liked being able to switch on an electric light once I'd got used to it but I was terrified of the gas. It took me a while to pluck up enough courage to strike a match and light a gas-jet. Everything seemed to happen so fast it fair took my breath away. When I wanted water I had only to turn on a tap and better still when I wanted to get rid of the water I needed to do no more than let it swill down the sink or drain instead of having to carry the pail or basin outside and sluice the water over the ground. Folks had told me about such things but I'd not been expecting to see them for myself. It was all such luxury it didn't seem natural. No carrying water from the well in all weathers. No peats to cut and stack and carry home but instead a coalman bringing bags of dusty coal with his horse and cart every week. Ach, I got used to it soon enough and I tried hard not to let folks see how strange I found everything.' Looking across at him she caught his perceptive nod.

'No doubt I myself would have felt the same, just,' he said.

'There's another thing that took me a whiley to get used to,' she continued, 'and that was their flush lavatories.' She permitted herself a tiny embarrassed chuckle. 'My but I'm saying they fairly made me flush scarlet and I mind I let myself get well and truly constipated before I

37

could bring myself to use one. Being used to having the whole stretch of the moors to choose my place I was shocked when I was shown the dark little cave of a wee hoosie in my aunt's back yard. There was no way you could disguise where you were going because there was nowhere else to go just. I thought it was a terrible lack of privacy even though there was a door you could shut. But when you'd finished there was this chain you had to pull and it fairly scared me out of my mind the first time I tried it for it made such a dreadful noise. Even when I got used to it I still used to be in an agony of shame because I was certain all the neighbours would hear it and say to themselves, "There's that strange girl from the Islands having to use the lavatory again". I got to pulling the chain and rushing out as fast as I could in the hope they wouldn't see it was me.'

She shook her head. 'And then there was only news-paper to clean yourself afterwards instead of a handful of good fresh moss. It didn't strike me as being clean or healthy.' She intercepted his nod of approbation.

'That's the city for you,' he said. 'Some folks think it cleaner but I doubt it myself.'

'Mind you,' she confided, 'it was my job to cut the newspapers into neat squares every Saturday night and then thread them on a piece of string and hang them from a nail on the lavatory door. I didn't dislike doing that because I got a good read of the papers while I was doing it and that was better than reading the Bible which was the only alternative.' She shot a glance at him to see if her light dismissal of the Bible had aroused a look of censure. His expression had not changed. She felt a sense of relief. The Islanders were known for their devoutness and though she had not relinquished her own strict religious upbringing – she would never have dared to speak of the Bible disparagingly in her Granny's time – the city had liberated her from much of its constraint. She had no wish to re-encounter it.

'After I'd had to leave my aunt's place I was taken on

by the minister and his wife and I got another surprise. I found their lavatory was inside on the upstairs landing and the chain made such a noise you could hear it all over the house. Well, I thought, you'd expect ministers' wives to be more particular about such things but no, they weren't bothered about it at all. They had a roll of toilet paper instead of newspaper but ach, it was that thin you could have spat through it. I'm telling you, my Granny would have suspected they were debauched,' she added with a giggle. She paused, shocked at her disclosures to a man she barely knew. 'Ach but I shouldn't be speaking to you of such things,' she excused herself. 'Likely it is the whisky that has let loose my tongue.'

He smiled appreciatively. 'It was good to hear you talk,' he said, helping himself to another scone. 'These are good!' he complimented her.

A glance at the yellowed face of the kitchen clock told Kirsty that they had been talking for well over an hour and a half and yet they were only a little nearer mentioning the subject they had met to discuss. She recognised a mounting tension within herself. There was so much more she must find out about him, her mind stressed but how was she to do it in the limited time before Isabel and Mac returned? She tried to devise some subtle comment that would serve to shape his mind in that direction but he forestalled her.

'The master and mistress of the house are out for the evening, you said. Will they be late back?'

'Shortly after midnight, I reckon,' she told him. 'I think they go to a cinema and afterwards they go for a drink with some of their friends.'

'Do you yourself go to the cinema?'

She gave a negative shake of her head. 'When I first came to the city I longed to go and see a picture. The cinemas looked so inviting with their bright lights and music whenever I went past them but the old aunt I was living with at the time said they were "Devil's Palaces" and I mustn't think of going inside one of them. The

39

Reverend MacDonald and his wife regarded them in much the same way and told me I should be ashamed of myself for mentioning the word "cinema" in such a place as the Manse. It wasn't until after I came here to work for Mrs Ross that I got the chance to go. Indeed, she herself took me to an afternoon matinée but I found it a sore disappointment. Ach, it was a cosy enough place but I caught fleas and I wasn't of a mind to pay sixpence to watch pictures and feed fleas so I didn't go again,' she said drily.

'You wouldn't miss such things, then?'

Her heart gave a little leap. He was on the edge of approaching the purpose of their meeting. 'I would not,' she assured him. 'Indeed there is very little the city offers that I should miss.' He noticed a small furrow of concentration appear between her eyes as if she was trying to recall some diversion she might miss. 'Maybe the swimming baths,' she admitted. 'I enjoy swimming but the baths are fast becoming so crowded and noisy I'm not much tempted to go these days.' She hesitated a moment. 'But I'm forgetting the public library. Now that is a place I should miss sadly. Ever since I learned to read I've loved books. My greatest pleasure is a good book.' She injected a note of seriousness into her voice so as not to lead him into thinking she might be persuaded to contemplate relinquishing such amenities.

'There is a good postal library to the Islands these days,' he was quick to tell her. 'It will send books regularly and you can keep them for a few weeks before you need send them back. And,' he emphasized, 'it's all paid for by the Education Authority.'

She was sceptical. There'd been nothing like that when she was young. 'What kind of books? Lesson books?' she queried.

'No indeed. My brother gets every kind of book for the asking. He's a rare man for reading once the outside work is finished and on the Sabbath whenever he can be alone.'

'Your brother lives on the Island?' His mention of a brother took her by surprise.

'My brother also lives in the house. It is the two of us just since the old folk passed on.'

She caught her breath. Sharing a house with two men was something she had not envisaged. She was immediately suspicious. 'Your brother,' she began haltingly. 'Is he in good health?' She could well understand Ruari Mac-Donald seeking a wife if there was an invalid brother dependent upon him.

'My brother is in the best of health,' he replied. 'He is a big man and he is altogether stronger and cleverer than myself. He has never seen a doctor and his teacher said he was such a good scholar he could have gone to University. He won bursaries but ach, he was never keen to go away from the Island.'

'Is he older or younger than yourself?'

'He is older by a year or two.'

'And he's never married?' The Islands were noted for their bachelors. 'Would there be a reason for that?'

'He's too content with his fishing and his sheep and his handiwork and his reading to have time for a woman, though there's many a good lassie would have been pleased to have the chance to marry him.'

This time it was she who noticed the slight crease furrowing his brow. She guessed that he was becoming sensitive to her questioning. But, she excused herself, she had to continue. There was so much she must know before she could consider giving him her decision. 'Are there no other crofters on your Island?' she pursued.

'Not a one. Not since many years back about the time of the evictions, my father used to say.'

'They were forced to go?'

'No, but the Laird at that time was so hard on them that they chose to go.'

'Those were cruel days,' she mused. 'I mind the old folk telling such sad stories at the ceilidhs ever since I was a wee bairn. They must have suffered terribly.'

'It was nigh on a hundred years ago,' he reminded her.

'My Granny used to tell me that her own Granny used to croon a sad song saying they were left with nothing but the burial ground,' she continued.

'But it was sorted after a while,' he soothed.

'It was a long enough while before it was sorted,' she contested. 'Folks still had bitter memories that had been told to them.'

'True,' he agreed. 'And I'm thinking life wasn't all that easy after the settlement. My own grandparents were poor enough. My father had to go and work as a herdboy for the Laird when he was very young and I mind him saying to us that the Laird was a mean and unjust man that would grudge him the wee bowl of oatmeal he'd get for his wages.' He frowned. 'But the time came when the Laird took to the gay life in the South and squandered all his money till he had to dispose of the whole estate including the Island.'

'I'd say it served him right,' Kirsty murmured.

'Aye, but the crofters were gey worried when they heard the new Laird was to be an Englishman I can tell you. But they need not have worried. He turned out to be a good and fair man and treated his employees and his tenants well enough. My father worked as a shepherd for him and was often enough on the Island to see to the sheep. He got to know it well and thought a lot of it. He had the Laird's son over on the Island with him one day and my father mentioned to him that it had been worked by the crofters until they abandoned it. When the Laird himself heard of it he immediately offered the Island to any crofters who were keen to go back there.'

'And did they?' she asked.

'Ach, they wouldn't listen to him. Folks were petitioning to be taken off the Islands at that time, not wanting to go and live on them.' After a short pause he went on, 'It was said it was mostly the womenfolk fearing they'd be too isolated that stopped the men from going.' He gave her a wavering smile before shaking his head. 'It was a pity right enough, seeing they would have had near three hundred acres of fairly good land they could have portioned among themselves. But no, they'd have none of it. They were all wanting easier crofts on the mainland.'

'I suppose one couldn't blame them for that, ' Kirsty commented. 'And yet your parents went there?'

'Well, how that came about was when the Laird's own son came of age he asked his father to give him the Island so he could try farming it himself. His father not only agreed but he built him a fine house with the stone from some of the old ruined cottages that had been abandoned. It was a good strong house, too, with three rooms and a kitchen, and a tiled roof rather than the thatch that was used at the time. It was newly finished just when the war broke out and the son went off to be an officer. The poor laddie never came back. My own father was in the war, too, but he wasn't even wounded and when he came back he had it in his mind that he wanted to marry my mother who was cook at the Laird's house on the mainland. When he spoke of his wish the Laird offered my father the Island and the house there as a wedding gift in recognition of his and my mother's loyal service.'

'He must have thought a lot of your parents,' Kirsty said.

'Aye, indeed he did. And the Laird's wife was almost like a sister to my mother, she used to say.'

'So they married and moved to the Island and lived happily ever after,' Kirsty concluded.

'Aye, but my father took a whiley to think about it before he accepted the Laird's offer,' he told her. 'See, he doubted my mother wouldn't marry him because she might want for company after being used to having the other workers around at the big house, but when he did put it to her she said she was prepared to go if that was what he wanted. Once they were married they ferried some cows and sheep and hens across to the Island and a few days later they had a good ceilidh for the wedding guests in their fine new house. I believe it was a great day indeed.'

'And were they happy there?' Kirsty enquired.

'I doubt if they ever regretted what they'd done,' he assured her. 'And that's where myself and my brother were born,' he added.

'Your schooling?' she probed.

'My father used to take us across the Sound every Monday morning so long as it was good enough weather.'

'To the mainland?'

'No, no, to another Island where there was a school and several scholars. Then he'd come for us on Friday evenings. If the weather was bad we'd stay with one of the crofters for the week-end. My mother often used to get across with him too so she'd be able to call and see her folks for a strupak.'

'And you say you have good water on your Island? Good wells and good peat hags and shelter for the animals?' Kirsty tried to make her tone sound congratulatory rather than inquisitive so he should not read too much interest into her questioning.

'We have very good water indeed on Westisle. Folks sometimes say they haven't tasted such good water and it makes a grand cup of tea,' he said glowingly. 'But the peat hags on the Island are shallow and the peat is poor under the kettle so we cut our peats on a small Island that's not so far away where there is more than plenty and no one to bother with it. We ferry it across in a flat-bottomed cattle boat we have that's grand for the peats just, and we can take all we need for the winter in no more than two loads.'

'Your brother is fond of fishing? Has he a fishing boat?'

'We have a fishing boat and mostly we fish together though I believe he is the better fisherman.'

'What is your fishing boat called?'

'It bears our joint names,' he told her.

'You haven't mentioned your brother's name,' she pointed out, suddenly realising that though they had been conversing companionably for more than two hours neither of them had used each other's Christian name.

'My brother's name is also Ruari,' he admitted with a shy grin and in response to her quizzically raised eyebrows he explained, 'See it was this way. My own father's favourite brother was our Uncle Ruari and when he went off to Canada my father told my mother that he wanted his first-born son to be named for him. That is why my brother is Ruari. My mother's father, that is my grandfather on her side was also named Ruari and she wanted a second son to be named for him. So when I was born I was also Ruari. My brother is Ruari Mhor seeing he's the eldest and I am Ruari Beag seeing I'm the youngest. Our fishing boat is named for the two of us: *The Two Ruaris*.'

'Of course, I'd forgotten how the old folk clung to the family names,' she observed with a wry smile.

He too smiled. 'The cattle ferry is also named *The Two Ruaris*,' he confided, his smile widening, 'but we have a small dinghy that has an outboard motor which is handy enough for just one of us to manage.'

'Now you're not going to tell me that the dinghy is also named for the two of you, surely?' she teased him archly.

'No, indeed. We named her *Katy* after our mother,' he answered gravely.

'How frequently do you get supplies and mail?' she asked.

'The boat calls twice a month with supplies and mails.'

'Only twice a month?' she echoed dubiously.

'But we don't depend on the boat just,' he hastened to tell her. 'When we take our fish to the mainland we can collect any mails and pick up anything we might be short of. We manage well enough.'

She tried to recall shortages in her Granny's time when snow had blocked roads or ferries had been harbour-bound by weather. 'Bread?' she asked. 'My Granny used to think it a great treat to get city bread from time to time.'

'Ach, we can get bread any time we're across. Not that

we eat so very much of it. My brother has no liking for city bread. Since my mother learned him how to make good girdle scones and bannocks, he spurns city bread even as a treat. No, we do not miss bread.'

'Your brother sounds a right "lad o pairts",' Kirsty complimented him. 'You tell me he is a good scholar and a good fisherman, a good shepherd and a good baker. Is there anything he is not good at?'

He'd rested his chin on his hand and had appeared to be considering deeply. 'He's not so good with the cattle,' he allowed. 'He gets mighty cross with them when they're being stupid and he miscalls them.' He glanced at her with a grin that had verged on the impish. 'Indeed the minister wouldn't be best pleased to hear the way he miscalls them sometimes.' His glance changed suddenly to one of anxiety as if he feared he might have shocked her. She treated him to a complaisant smile.

'It's the cattle just he miscalls,' he resumed. 'You'd never hear a bad word from him at any other time. Mostly it's myself sees to the cattle except at sale time when it needs the two of us to round them up.' She nodded. 'And he doesn't take much to do with the hens, so I see to those myself. But he is good with his brain and with his hands. It's himself that made much of the furniture in the house from good pieces of driftwood we have found on the shore from time to time, and didn't he repair the water tank, the one which the Laird had built beside the burn with the idea that his son would have water piped down to the house. The tank had leaked for a while and the piping was rusty and broken in places. My father had taken no heed of it, being always used to carrying water from the burn or the well but my brother wasn't finished with school before he had it sorted. My mother was never tired of praising him for that, seeing she no longer had to carry pails of water.'

'You're saying you have water from a tap like there is in the city?' There was scepticism in her tone.

'Indeed we have so,' he asserted and smiled at her expectantly.

She again looked at the kitchen clock before rising from her chair. 'I must take the guests their evening tea and biscuits,' she said, knowing, and guessing that he also knew, that she was stalling for time before giving him her decision.

While she was preparing the trays and taking them into the Smoking Room her mind occupied itself with assessing what Ruari MacDonald was offering her. A good house, he'd promised, and she was prepared to believe him; a regular supply of milk and eggs, of fish, of fresh water and of peats. It sounded like all the necessities for a fairly comfortable life, but if he was to be her man what else would she want of him? Could she grow fond of him? Was she willing to try? While there was nothing about him that in any way repelled her, neither was there anything that kindled more than a feeling of leniency towards him. At their age and after so short an acquaintance affection was fanciful, she told herself, but what had drawn him to her? What would he be wanting of her? Loyalty in response to his offers she would be prepared to give but would she be willing to share his bed if that was what he wanted? A tiny quiver of excitement told her she would not be too averse to the idea; she dared to let herself think it might be endurable, possibly even pleasant. She smothered the thought hastily. It must be made quite clear to him that she was almost certainly too old to bear children. But not yet, she wavered.

When she returned to the kitchen he was looking at the newspaper which Mac had left.

'Will I make another pot of tea?' she asked him.

'Aye,' he agreed, 'that will be welcome.' He put away the paper and watched her while she made the tea and poured out two cups. Then with only a slight preliminary clearing of his throat he asked, 'Will I speak to the minister here tomorrow about us?'

Kirsty knew there was one final question she must put

47

to him before she could agree. Falteringly she asked, 'Your brother, will he be sore at you for asking a woman to share your house?'

'My brother will take no more to do with you than you'd wish,' he assured her.

She looked up at him critically while she again asked herself if she was being sensible; if leniency could be a substitute for affection?

'Will I do that just?' he pressed.

Kirsty lowered her eyes. 'You will do that,' she'd consented. He stretched out a hand but only far enough along the table to take her glass. 'Oh, no more than a wee sippie,' she bade him and since the bottle was almost empty he found it easy enough to comply.

Standing up he raised his glass to his lips. 'To Kirsty *mho ghaoil*!' he proclaimed.

She raised her glass similarly. 'To Ruari Beag MacDonald!' she returned but she was too shy to add any endearment.

Thus with no more than a dram, a smile and a handshake the compact had been made.

It had been after four o'clock in the afternoon of the following day before she'd encountered Ruari MacDonald again. The house had been quiet, with Mac at work, Isabel at one of her almost daily whist-drives and Meggy out on an errand to the electric shop to get the wireless accumulators recharged. None of the guests were due back until shortly before the evening meal so she'd planned to wash out a few 'smalls', but before doing so she'd looked into the Smoking Room to check Meggy had banked up the fire ready for the evening. There she had found him sitting in an armchair near the window with the daily paper covering his lap, evidently having slipped from his hands, and his head lolling against the anti-macassar which covered the chair back. She'd guessed he was snoozing and since the fire needed no attention was about to withdraw quietly when she heard him call abruptly, '*Tha e Fuar!*'

'*He Fooar!*' she responded immediately, before reverting to the English. 'Indeed it is cold. I wonder you are not sitting nearer the fire.'

'I am meaning it is cold outside this house,' he explained. 'It is not cold in here.' He'd seemed unsure how to continue the conversation.

'I was just after checking to see there was a good fire going,' she told him and after a second or two's pause asked, 'You will be feeling like a strupak?' She hadn't really wanted to go back into the kitchen to make a strupak at this moment, having only a few minutes previously finished her own leisurely cup of tea but she'd felt a need to say something inconsequential and the traditional enquiry had shaped itself effortlessly to her tongue. He gestured grateful acceptance but as she turned to go he rose from his chair and stepped hurriedly to waylay her.

49

'I have seen the minister,' he advised in a low voice. 'He will be willing to marry us the day after tomorrow.'

'On Thursday?' she exclaimed, her eyes widening in disbelief. 'That isn't possible. It is much too soon!'

'Was I not after telling you I need to be back on Westisle for the cattle sale on Thursday next,' he reminded her firmly. 'We shall need to be away from here no later than Tuesday to be certain of reaching the Island by then.'

'But I cannot leave here on Tuesday.' The denial escaped from her lips in a shocked whisper and, seeing his puzzled expression she added hastily, 'You don't understand about these things. I am required to give a week's notice before I can leave here.'

He looked at her, a little pityingly she thought, and appeared to dismiss her protest. 'Seeing I was nearby I called in at the railway station to book for you a ticket. I myself have the other half of the return ticket which brought me here.'

She felt momentarily breathless. 'But I shall not be able to travel with you then,' she insisted but even as she spoke she was conscious of a degree less conviction in her tone as a sudden vindictiveness darted, unbidden, into her mind. Wouldn't it serve Isabel right if she left without giving due warning? And since she was intending to cut her links with *ISLAY* sooner or later why shouldn't she cut them suddenly? Isabel deserved neither loyalty nor consideration and her own loyalty now must surely be to the man whom she was pledged to marry. And wasn't the day after tomorrow the day she was due her afternoon and evening off anyway? Apart from the rush he couldn't have fixed a more suitable time.

She felt him watching her keenly, no doubt waiting for her to reveal whatever was passing through her mind. Drawing a deep breath she looked straight at him. 'I will be ready to go with you to Westisle on Tuesday as you wish,' she said resolutely, 'but neither of us must say one word about the matter until that day.'

'That will be the way of it,' he confirmed, touching her shoulder lightly.

When she took his strupak into the Smoking Room she put an extra cup on the tray for herself. She could always drink a cup of tea in company no matter how many she might have drunk previously. There was still so much she wanted to find out about him and this seemed a good opportunity.

After they'd been talking casually for a few minutes she said, 'Tell me, do Island women work as hard these days as I remember my Granny working when I was a girl? I'm meaning outside work.'

'Ach, I'd say there is not so much,' he said dismissively. 'Maybe the hens and the milking and the calf feeding.' He paused for only a second before adding, 'But only if they have a mind that way.'

'I should be willing to see to the hens and the milking and calf feeding since those things my Granny taught me to do and I daresay I could lend a hand at planting and harvest time, but I would not wish to be at the sheep dipping or the shearing and nor would I care to be at the calf cutting.' He seemed to realise she was voicing not a wish but a refusal.

'That is all men's work,' he snorted. 'I doubt you would be needed or welcome at such times. My brother and myself have always managed these things without help.'

After another short silence she said, 'I will need to get myself a portmanteau. There is very little I would wish to take from here but there will be some things.'

'Just so,' he assented. 'Will I get a portmanteau for you and keep it in my bedroom? It would not look strange for me to do that seeing I am to be leaving soon enough.'

'That would be the best way,' she agreed, nodding her head in approval. 'But you must promise to tell me the cost so I can give you the necessary money.'

'Ach, there will be no need for you to do that,' he demurred.

'But you must take the money,' she insisted proudly.

She wasn't going to have him thinking she would allow him to spend money on her before they had made their marriage vows.

Immediately divining the reason for her insistence he slanted her a faintly roguish smile. 'I will not buy the portmanteau until after we are wed,' he promised her. She treated him to a spectral nod of acceptance, feeling curiously relieved, not so much because there would be no need for her to dip into her own small savings but because his conduct had banished her uncertainty about his attitude to money. She knew Island men were as a rule sensible about money matters but she'd heard stories of the odd one or two who were so 'money hungry' their dependents suffered miserably. Ruari MacDonald was plainly not one of them, she concluded.

She felt even more assured when the next moment he said, 'I will need to buy a ring for you to wear, will I not? A gold wedding ring?' She looked speculatively at her bare hands resting in her lap. 'Is that not the way of it?' She acknowledged his question with a grave smile. 'How am I to know the thickness of your finger?' he asked. There was a hint of eagerness in his tone. 'You will take time to meet me at the jeweller's shop?'

'That I do not intend to do,' she told him. 'I believe it is not the custom, but I will take the measure of my finger with a piece of wool,' she promised him. 'I've heard tell it is the way it is done,' she added quickly in case he should think she was speaking from previous experience. As his lips shaped to ask a further question she forestalled him by saying, 'I will leave the piece of wool on the tray on top of the dressing table in your bedroom.'

Just at that moment she glimpsed Meggy passing the window, and then heard the thump of the back door and felt the draught as it opened and closed. Rising from the chair she said, 'I must away now and set Meggy to preparing the vegetables.' He looked at her questioningly as she picked up the tray.

'Will I come to the kitchen tonight?' he asked.

'Not tonight. We could not be sure of having it to ourselves.'

'You will not forget about the wool?' he called after her as she was leaving the room.

'I will not forget the wool,' she assured him with a coy grin.

That same evening in her bedroom she took her few clothes out of the wardrobe and inspected them carefully. It would be nice to buy something new for her wedding, she thought, but what money she'd managed to save she was not going to squander on clothes which might not be suitable for Island wear even supposing she could take the time off to go shopping for them. She held up her Harris tweed suit on its hanger. It was almost new and looked in as fresh a condition as it had looked on the day when it had been given to her by a young woman who'd stayed briefly at *ISLAY* while en route to Gibraltar where she was to marry and settle down. The young woman had told her she had been a schoolteacher on the Isle of Lewis; her fiancé had lived in Edinburgh but had now been transferred to Gibraltar, from where he'd written to say she would need only lightweight clothes for the climate there so the suit was something she could very well dispense with. Observing that they were of similar build, the young woman had suggested Kirsty should try it on. The suit had fitted perfectly with the result that Kirsty had been persuaded to accept it as a gift. She'd used it only for church-going on fine Sundays and consequently it had seen very little wear.

Satisfied that it was ideal for a wedding at this time of year, she returned the suit to the wardrobe and took out her cherished Burberry. Ever since she had seen the Laird's wife and guests wearing what her Granny had described as 'Grand Folks Cotamors', which she had subsequently come to know as Burberrys, she had aspired to wear one herself. It had taken her years to save for one and it was already several winters old but she had taken great care of it, as she had of all her clothes and it still looked as good as new. Her problem, as she saw it, was that the Burberry was not roomy enough to wear over her suit jacket. Her suit jacket, on the other hand, was not waterproof. She wished she could still 'read the sky' as her Granny had taught her to do, but since she'd come to the city she'd seen so little of the sky her aptitude had waned from lack of practice. All she could do now was to resign herself to waiting to see how the day after tomorrow should dawn, weatherwise before she would know what she should wear. If it was wet it must be the Burberry over the skirt of the suit and her prettiest jersey. If it looked reasonably fine she would wear the suit and as a precaution take the light macintosh she used when nipping out on short errands such as visits to the local library. It was a trifle shabby but unless the weather turned really wet she would keep it draped over her arm.

Finally she inspected her one and only hat and her Sunday shoes. The hat – a soft black cloche of which old Mrs Ross had tired – she had to admit looked somewhat defeated, but she reckoned it could be enlivened by a judicious steaming and pressing. She twirled the hat in her hand, grimacing at it as she did so. She'd always rebelled at wearing hats and had shunned the thought of spending money on them. When she'd needed to confine her hair she wore a black chenille tammy which she'd knitted from an old shawl, again one of Mrs Ross's cast-offs, which she'd unravelled. Her shoes had also seen their best days but she'd made a habit of keeping them so well polished that they didn't betray their cheapness.

Kirsty sat on her bed assessing how she would look in either outfit and accepted with a rueful smile that though she would not look exactly bridal, neither would she disgrace her wedding-day by looking like a tinker. Pulling open a drawer, she looked at the three clean and neatly folded wincyette nightdresses it contained, one floral, one pink, and one white all with lace trimming round the neck and sleeves. Thank goodness she'd always made a point of wearing pretty nightdresses, she thought. For a few moments she stared at them reflectively and then pushing the drawer firmly shut she got quickly into bed.

She waited until Meggy had finished cleaning the bedrooms next morning before nipping up to Ruari MacDonald's room to put the small finger-sized piece of wool on a tray as she'd promised. When she returned to the kitchen Meggy's first remark was, 'How much longer is that Mr MacDonald booked in for? D'you know when he's supposed to be going back to his Island?'

For an instant Kirsty was startled into suspecting there might have been some form of thought transference but she managed to reply offhandedly, 'One day next week, I believe. Why do you ask?'

'Oh, it's just that I'll be sorry to see the last of him,' Meggy said as she ran hot water into the sink in preparation for washing dusters. 'I could wish we got more folks like him at ISLAY,' she continued. 'He's a real nice gentleman. Never a cross word from him and never leaves his bedroom untidy like most other men. And he never uses the chamber pot, or if he does he empties it himself. Not like some,' she grumbled. 'Honest, you'd swear they spend half the night peeing instead of sleeping.'

Kirsty chuckled and hurriedly made as much noise as she could while replenishing the fire with coals. She had no wish to embark on a discussion of Ruari MacDonald's habits good or bad at this stage but it was comforting to know that at least he'd won Meggy's approval. Remembering Meggy was due to take part of the afternoon off she asked, 'Meggy, is there a chance of you calling at the draper's this afternoon? I could do with a new pair of stockings and the nearest shop I can get to closes this afternoon.'

'Yes I'll get them at the shop near our house,' Meggy offered. 'I believe he's a halfpenny cheaper with most things than the one you go to. Is it the usual grey or will I get you some flesh coloured and cheer your legs up a bit?'

'Grey,' Kirsty said firmly. 'You know perfectly well I only ever wear grey or black.'

'More fool you,' retorted Meggy. 'When somebody's got nice legs they ought to show them off a bit. That's what my mother says.'

'And have I got nice legs?' Kirsty put the question indifferently.

'The greengrocer says you have.'

'That rascal!' exclaimed Kirsty witheringly.

The greengrocer came weekly, his horse-drawn cart creaking under its load of fruit and vegetables but though she welcomed the freshness and cheapness of his produce his foul language and his persistent attempts to flirt with her made her shudder. She'd shuddered even more when she'd learned he was a respected member of the church which, among her acquaintances, was invariably alluded to as 'Dommed Papist'.

At that moment Isabel came into the kitchen carrying a frilled blouse which she put down on the table. 'I want this ironing for tonight,' she announced, 'and make sure you don't singe it.' Kirsty merely glanced at the garment. 'It's tussore so you'll need to take great care. Don't leave it to her,' she added, with a derisive glance at Meggy.

'She won't leave it to me because I'm due to go off from one o'clock until three this afternoon,' Meggy told her pertly.

'Well, see you're back on time,' Isabel warned.

She was about to leave the kitchen when Kirsty said, 'Isabel, we're really getting very short of butter for the guests. I did mention it to you a couple of days ago but you haven't ordered any and we really shan't last out until the grocer comes again.'

'There's cooking margarine, isn't there?' Isabel demanded.

'Yes, of course, but you can't surely . . . ?'

Isabel cut short Kirsty's protest. 'There's no reason why you shouldn't mix it with what butter we have left. They'll not be likely to notice the difference.' Seeing Kirsty's expression of dismay she went on, 'We'll have to do some detectivising and find out where all the butter goes to these days.' Her eyes slid meaningfully towards Meggy's back.

'Start looking in your larder,' Meggy advised her saucily. 'It wouldn't surprise me if you've got a whole brigade of rats in there.'

'Don't be ridiculous,' Isabel snapped and left the kitchen.

'Meggy!' Kirsty reproved her warningly.

Meggy tittered quietly. 'She's a narky old besom,' she said.

As soon as Meggy had gone Kirsty lit the gas-iron and placed the ironing pad on the table and after she'd pressed Isabel's blouse she brought down her own clothes and gave them a final pressing before taking them back to her room. She stood for a moment surveying them and then took out a pair of plain black gloves and a crisp white hankerchief from her knick-knack box and placed them on her dressing table. Satisfied she could make no further preparations for her wedding-day she went down to the kitchen.

Sleep that night came fitfully and it was with a sigh of relief she heard the alarm clock signal that it was time the kitchen fire was lit and breakfast preparations got under way. She made her own early morning cup of tea and started to prepare the porridge expecting Meggy to arrive at any moment to lay the tables in the dining room but half an hour later Meggy had still not arrived. Kirsty went through to the dining room and lit the gasfire, and after another half hour had passed and still no Meggy she herself began to set out the tables for the guests' breakfast. She became anxious. Had Meggy met with an accident? Should Isabel be told? She glanced at the clock. Isabel would be expecting Meggy to be bringing her early morning tea in five minutes. She waited another five minutes before taking up the tray.

'Where's Meggy?' Isabel demanded sleepily.

57

'I'm afraid she isn't here yet,' Kirsty told her. 'Something must have delayed her. She didn't say anything last night about not coming in so I daresay she'll be here soon.'

'She'd better be,' Isabel said grumpily.

But Meggy had still not turned up when Kirsty was due to leave for her afternoon off. Isabel came into the kitchen. 'That good-for-nothing still not here?' she burst out irascibly. 'I suppose it's no good telling you to give up your afternoon and have it tomorrow instead?'

'No, what I have to do today will not wait until tomorrow,' Kirsty told her firmly. 'The meal is well prepared so you should not have much to do.'

'But I wanted to bring some of my friends here this afternoon for a game of whist,' Isabel grumbled. 'And I wanted Meggy to see to the fire in the Smoking Room and to bring us in some tea and biscuits.'

Kirsty merely raised her eyebrows. 'Too bad!' she murmured relentlessly. 'I expect she'll be in soon,' she comforted, but Isabel had already left the kitchen.

Up in her room Kirsty dressed carefully. The morning had looked settled enough but though there was now rather more grey in the sky, she decided she would be safe in wearing her suit livened up with a Cairngorm brooch her aunt had given her and carrying her mac over her arm. She had arranged to meet Ruari MacDonald outside the public library as near to three o'clock as she could manage so, at ten minutes to three she let herself quietly out of the front door of *ISLAY* and walked briskly in that direction.

The minister was waiting for them at the Manse and, giving the impression that he was anxious to get on with the ceremony, he bustled them into the church where, after introducing them to his wife and the verger he began to read the wedding service. They made their solemn promises: the ring slid onto her finger; the blessing was given and they signed the register. The minister then did justice to the expected half bottle of whisky Ruari had produced from his pocket, wiped his mouth thoroughly on his handkerchief and then ushered them out of the church and back to the Manse where, at his wife's invitation they stayed for a cup of tea and a scone that Kirsty thought was so stale she would have thrown it out for the birds.

It was all over bewilderingly quickly and when they came out on the street again a thin drizzle had already started. Not sure what to do with themselves they went into one of the big stores, took the lift to the top floor and then walked down the flights of stairs to the ground floor again. People were rushing in, lowering their umbrellas as they came through the swing doors, their clothes limp with rain. They entered another store where an enterprising department head was directing some of his staff to make a display of umbrellas conveniently near to the exit. Ruari MacDonald stopped.

'I will buy you an umbrella for a wedding present,' he offered.

'No, no, you shall not!' she forbade him. Surely he realised how useless an umbrella would be on a windswept Island? But he was already selecting an umbrella and paying the assistant.

'I have not yet bought you a wedding present Bheinn Ruari MacDonald,' he bent to speak into her ear because of the street noises and the chattering voices of shoppers around them. She felt her cheeks grow warm but made no comment. Through her wet gloves she twisted the gold ring on her finger. Bheinn Ruari MacDonald! She liked the sound. The wife of Ruari MacDonald. No longer would she need describe herself as 'Kirsty MacLennan, spinster'. The knowledge seeping into her mind made her oblivious of the rain seeping through her clothes until her new husband said, 'Will you not put up your umbrella?'

'It is too wild to risk that,' she objected. 'I will put on my macintosh.' He held the umbrella while she struggled with her macintosh, and when he handed it back to her their eyes met for an instant and they exchanged a wisp of a smile.

'You would like to go into a tea shop and have a wee strupak?' he coaxed, but she would not.

'We must not risk being seen together,' she reminded him. He nodded. The weather was worsening rapidly and she went on, 'I'm thinking we would be wise to go back to *ISLAY*.'

'Not to a hotel?' Her startled expression made him add, 'for a meal just.'

'The weather could be even coarser in a couple of hours,' she warned him.

'Very well,' he accepted. 'We will go back to *ISLAY*.'

And that is how the man and the woman came to be walking in their silent separate-togetherness through the wind and the rain and the sleet, the woman with a new gold ring on her finger, her only wedding present – the umbrella – still tightly furled under her arm and her mind still wondering if there were many women who had received – and accepted – such a strange proposal and had experienced such a singular wedding day.

The morning after her wedding Kirsty rose at her usual time and went down to the kitchen to begin her morning chores. She was making the breakfast porridge when the kitchen door opened and the errant Meggy appeared.

'Here I am!' Meggy announced and then straightway went on to ask, 'Was Her Ladyship in a terrible dander when I didn't turn up yesterday?' Her tone was in no way contrite.

Kirsty looked at her searchingly. 'She was certainly not very pleased,' she said. 'But what happened to stop you coming? Are you all right? I was worried about you, fearing you'd had an accident or something.'

'Oh, I'm all right,' Meggy assured her. 'But I had to stay at home because of this boil on my dad's bum. No, honest!' she continued, aware of Kirsty's raised eyebrows. 'You remember I was telling you about it the day before yesterday? Well, it was swelling so big he had to have the nurse come twice a day to treat it, and he couldn't go to work because she said he must lie in bed until it burst. Then yesterday morning just as Mam was setting off for her job at the laundry he gave a great yell to say the thing was near bursting and he must have the nurse come straight away to see to it. Well Mam always managed to be at home when the nurse came before but she said she daren't take any more time off for fear she'd get the sack. She said right enough she'd call and tell the nurse on her way to the laundry but that I'd have to stay home because she wasn't going to have the nurse treating her man's bum when he'd be in the house by himself.' She studied Kirsty's expression. 'Well, I did have to stay, didn't I?' she pleaded.

'I suppose you did under the circumstances,' Kirsty

allowed with a grin. 'But I'm just surprised he needed the nurse at all. I'd have thought your mother could have done all that was necessary. I know a boil is a nasty, painful thing but it's not very serious after all.'

'It is when it's on a man's backside,' argued Meggy. 'And it was a terrible big one,' she enthused. 'Mam was feared it might disable him or something. Anyway Mam's not much good when it comes to first aid. She can't stand the sight of blood and she'd have been more likely to faint right off if she'd tried to do anything with it – even supposing he'd have let her go near it. He's a right coward himself sometimes.' Meggy tied on her apron and filled the cutlery basket ready to take through into the dining room. She paused by the door. 'Was the old scarecrow really blowing steam about me not coming in yesterday?' she pressed.

'Of course she was,' Kirsty told her. 'You wouldn't expect her to be anything else would you? She'll probably give you a row and threaten the sack but we managed quite well without you so she doesn't really have much to grumble about.'

Meggy tossed her head. 'I'm well used to her giving me a row,' she said.

'Actually the worst upset was because your not being here stopped them from going to a film they'd planned to go and see.'

'How would that stop them?' Meggy queried, a puzzled frown creasing her brow.

'You weren't here, were you, to see to the hot water bottles and the late teas.'

'But you were here, surely?'

'Oh, indeed I was but it was my evening off, remember.'

'Yes, I know it was but you hardly ever take your evening off and you wouldn't have minded doing those two little things if they'd asked you, would you? I mean, you've never minded before.'

'That's just the point,' Kirsty enlightened her. 'I wasn't

asked last night, I was just told to do it so I turned thrawn and insisted on having the whole evening off. Isabel herself had to stay and see to the guests.'

Meggy's mouth dropped open with shock. 'You never did!' she ejaculated, plonking the cutlery basket down on the table as if she needed all her strength to take in Kirsty's startling disclosure.

'I did indeed,' Kirsty affirmed. 'I just felt I'd had enough of the pair of them taking it for granted that I'd be willing to give up my free time whenever they wanted to go off and enjoy themselves. Never once have they spoken a word of thanks to me so I decided it was high time they were taught a lesson.' She became aware that simply telling Meggy what she had done had given her a small feeling of elation. She almost wished she could divulge the rest of the news.

Meggy's eyes glinted with excitement. 'Hurrah!' she rejoiced. 'I never would have thought you had it in you.' She was still chuckling as she picked up the cutlery basket and tripped off into the dining room.

A moment or two later Mac, clad in his working clothes, poked his head round the door of the kitchen. 'Has that wench come into work this morning?' he demanded in a voice that was roughened by smoker's croak.

'She's in the dining room,' Kirsty told him.

'Isa's got a headache,' he announced. 'She's staying in bed for a whiley till she feels better. See that wench doesn't go banging about upstairs and upsetting her.' Kirsty threw him a distasteful glance and let his remarks pass without comment. Treating her to a baleful glare he banged the kitchen door shut and hurried out to the backyard gate.

When Meggy came back into the kitchen she asked, 'Was that the Hooligan I heard you talking to a minute ago?' Meggy invariably referred to Mac as the Hooligan.

'It was indeed,' Kirsty admitted flippantly. 'He came to say Isabel's got one of her headaches and intends to lie abed this morning. He says we're to be careful not to make a noise when we go upstairs so we shan't disturb her.'

'Oh dear,' sniggered Meggy. 'Was the poor wee thing overdoing the whisky again last night and now thinks she's hearing elephants plodding around the bedroom? Likely it was the whisky gave her the headache and she'll be taking more to cure it. My, but have you ever seen the number of bottles she hides under her bed?' Kirsty nodded. 'She'll drink herself daft,' declared Meggy with great satisfaction.

'More than likely,' agreed Kirsty.

When Isabel eventually appeared Kirsty and Meggy were having their regular morning break for a cup of tea. She scowled at Meggy. 'Where did you get to yesterday, I'd like to know?' she asked sharply as she poured herself a cup of tea from the pot.

'I stayed at home to look after my dad,' retorted Meggy. 'Kirsty says you managed okay without me.'

'You should have let me know,' carped Isabel.

'I couldn't since you haven't got a telephone and my brother would have been late for school if I'd sent him with a note.'

Kirsty thought Meggy sounded unusually defiant.

'And what's the matter with your dad that your mother couldn't look after him?' Isabel demanded to know, scepticism already edging her tone.

'My dad's in bed and my mother had to go to her job at the laundry,' said Meggy.

'And your mother's job at the laundry is so much more important than your job here?' Isabel asked cuttingly.

'Oh, yes,' Meggy retorted. 'She gets much better pay than I get here, and she gets more time off.'

Kirsty was baffled by the girl's brazen manner. She'd always been under the impression that what Meggy earned at ISLAY was desperately needed to supplement the family income, but now she appeared to be oblivious of the risk of offending her employer and losing her job. Kirsty grew tense as she waited for Isabel's reaction.

'That's enough of your cheek,' Isabel exploded. 'You can take a week's notice as from today. I can easily find someone to do what little work you do here – and do it better.'

A flash of consternation drove Kirsty to protest, 'Oh, Isabel! Do think again. Meggy's a good worker and I . . .' she curbed her tongue only just in time to stop herself from revealing that she herself would be leaving ISLAY the following Tuesday morning. Guilt attached itself to her consternation. She really should have given Isabel fair warning so as to allow her more time to look for another cook, she reproved herself but in the next instant Isabel's reply dislodged all traces of guilt.

'As for you, you can just shut your mouth and keep it shut so long as you're under my roof or you'll get the same treatment,' she raged. She emptied the dregs of her tea into the sink and put down her cup and saucer with such clumsy haste that Kirsty wondered they didn't shatter.

'You couldn't do without her even if you can do without me,' Meggy challenged as Isabel strode out of the kitchen, and when there was no response she ran to the kitchen door and shouted upstairs, 'You'd be a fool to try!'

'Meggy!' Kirsty admonished her. 'For goodness sake don't make things worse for yourself. Jobs aren't all that easy to find.'

'I've got another job already,' Meggy boasted. 'I was only waiting until Monday to give her my notice.'

'But if you upset her even more she might not give you a reference,' Kirsty pointed out.

'My Mam got me a job at the same place as herself so I don't need a reference.'

'You're going to work at the laundry?' Kirsty asked her. 'Will you like that?'

'Not much I daresay but I don't like my job here, so what? I'll miss your good cooking though,' Meggy added. 'The wages are better but you don't even get a cup of tea at the laundry, Mam says. All the same I'm going from here as soon as I get my wages.'

'When are your wages due to you?'

'Tomorrow, the end of the month,' Meggy gloated. 'And once I've got them in my pocket she won't see me again in this place.'

'You're planning to leave tomorrow?' There was a note of panic in Kirsty's voice.

'I'm going the minute I get my wages, notice or no notice,' asserted Meggy. 'You won't split on me, will you?' Seeing Kirsty's hurt expression she added repentantly, 'No, of course you won't – I'm daft to ask.'

The ringing of the Smoking Room bell sent Meggy hurrying from the kitchen and, left to herself for a moment, Kirsty had time to think of Isabel's predicament when, on Monday morning, she would discover she had neither a maid nor a cook-housekeeper. Meggy, Kirsty thought would be easy enough to replace. There were plenty of young girls who would be glad to get a job which also included a good dinner every day, but finding a new cook might take longer. Or had Isabel already someone in mind, she asked herself. Could that be the reason for her increasing hostility? She shrugged the query from her mind. She would soon get used to the fact that it no longer mattered.

When Meggy returned to the kitchen she said, 'I think you were right about that Mr MacDonald leaving early next week because he's just brought in two portmanteaux and taken them up to his room. I reckon he must have been doing a fair bit of shopping while he's been here.' She added after a moment's thought, 'I suppose he'd need to, wouldn't he?'

'They have only the bundles the tinkers bring around once or twice a year to choose from otherwise. Either that or buying from the catalogues,' Kirsty confirmed.

Meggy wrinkled her nose. 'I wouldn't fancy buying stuff from tinkers' bundles,' she said.

'Oh, but they have quite nice stuff very often. Mind

66

you, it's carried from house to house and village to village for so long it can be quite shop-soiled before you get a look at it. But my Granny always bought her nighties and semmits from the tinkers and my Uncle Donny's long underpants and my knickers. Folks looked forward to the coming of the tinkers. They were a sure sign that spring was coming. Every crofthouse welcomed them and every wifie bought something from them, whether it was a new kettle or a new pair of breeks. It tempted them to buy when they could get a look at the things before they bought them. Much better than just seeing illustrations or reading descriptions in dull catalogues. And you see Meggy, the tinkers brought not only their bundles full of goods but tongues full of news and gossip from the other places they'd visited on their travels, so folks found them sort of refreshing.'

'I could never abide to live on an Island where there were no shops, could you? I know you did when you were young but you wouldn't want to go back now you've got so used to living in the city, would you?' Meggy enquired.

'I sometimes wonder,' Kirsty temporised, again suppressing a near-compulsive desire to acquaint Meggy with her own plans.

On the Saturday after the evening meal had been cleared away and the kitchen tidied, Isabel came into the kitchen and put Meggy's due pay on the table. 'I've a good mind to keep this back until you've worked your week's notice,' she said grudgingly to Meggy. 'But see and don't you be late in the morning to serve the breakfast or I'll not reconsider and you'll get no wages for the week.'

Meggy looked at Kirsty and gave her a cocky smile from behind her hand. She made no mention to Isabel of her impending desertion. Evidently Meggy's mind was made up. With her wages safely in her pocket she was simply going to walk out of ISLAY and never come back. She shed a few tears when she took her leave of Kirsty that night but otherwise appeared as happy as a lark at finishing with her job at ISLAY. Kirsty would have liked to think that when Tuesday morning came she herself would be able to leave *ISLAY* with as light a heart.

On her way up to her bedroom that night Kirsty tapped lightly on the door of her new husband's bedroom. They had not had a chance to be alone nor even to speak to each other for more than a few snatched moments since they'd returned to *ISLAY* on their wedding day, and those few moments had been mostly hamstrung by embarrassment, but Meggy's reference to the two portmanteaux gave her the courage to seek a few words with Ruari now. The door opened and shyly he invited her into his room to inspect the portmanteaux and when she'd smiled her approval he carried one of them up the short flight of stairs to her attic room.

'I have made the last of the arrangements,' he told her in an undertone. 'The driver of the taxi has said he will surely be here by ten o'clock on Tuesday morning.'

'A taxi?' She was surprised at his extravagance but did not question it.

'Indeed,' he confirmed. 'You can be ready by that hour? It will cost more to keep him waiting on us,' he added shrewdly.

'I shall be ready. Even more than ready,' she promised him and after a whispered, *'Oidhche Mhath!'* a brief handclasp and an equally brief moment of eye contact, he turned and went back down the stairs.

As soon as the door had closed behind him she began to pack her clothes into the portmanteau along with the few cherished possessions she wished not to leave behind: her Bible which had been given to her by the minister's wife; an old sepia photograph of a troop of gloomy looking uniformed soldiers captioned *The Wet Review*, which her Granny had bade her treasure because one of the soldiers had been a relative of hers; a purple glass netfloat which her Uncle Donny had given her and a lump of wood which had been either carved or moulded by the sea into a shape that was curiously like a kneeling man bearing a heavy burden on his back. She herself had found the figure washed up on the shore but her Granny had told her it might be a 'wicked idol' that would bring bad luck and had wanted her to throw it back in the sea. Unaccountably she'd kept it, and by the time she'd left for the city the figure had acquired an air of permanency so she'd taken it with her wherever she went.

Tracking around the room, her eye lit on the small wireless set which Mrs Ross had given her and which had been her main source of relaxation. The earphones lay neatly beside it. With a slight catch of her breath she stared at it. Would Westisle be too remote to have wireless reception? Would she be able to get accumulators charged there? She sighed. It was just another of the questions she had omitted to ask Ruari, but their meetings had been so restricted, and the time for questioning and cross-questioning so limited, she excused herself.

As she had vowed, Meggy did not put in an appearance on Sunday morning but since there were only three boarders Kirsty coped easily both with breakfast and with dinner, which was always served mid-day on Sundays so as to enable staff to attend church. Isabel and Mac never came down for Sunday dinner so Kirsty decided that staying to do a batch of baking and so lighten Isabel's task, if only for the time it would take her to find a new cook, might do more to salve her own conscience than going to church. She was in the middle of cooking when Isabel, sour-faced and smoking a cigarette, came into the kitchen. Kirsty gave her an abrupt 'Good morning!' She had taken Isabel and Mac their morning tea at the usual time but they had been too sluggish with sleep to be aware that it was she and not Meggy who was in attendance.

Isabel looked around the kitchen. 'Where's that little bitch?' she snapped.

'I can't say,' Kirsty told her coolly.

'Has she been in at all this morning?'

'I haven't seen her.'

'Well if you haven't seen her she hasn't been in, has she?' Isabel snarled. 'Mac warned me I was a fool to pay

69

her wages last night and he was right. He's always telling me I'm too soft with people. I should have made her wait till next week and then paid her off for good.'

She slumped down on a chair. 'Any tea in that pot?' she asked grouchily. Kirsty brewed a pot of tea and handed her a cup. 'Not going to church?' Isabel remarked incuriously.

'Not today,' Kirsty said.

'In that case there's no need for me and Mac to stay in and mind the place,' Isabel said, stifling a yawn. 'There'll be little enough for you to do so you'll manage without Meggy.' There was only the barest trace of interrogation in her tone. Kirsty wanted to turn and point out that she had managed countless times before but she knew it would be a waste of breath and it might result in Isabel prolonging her visit to the kitchen which was something she was keen enough to avoid. Once Isabel and Mac had gone out for the rest of the afternoon she planned to ask Ruari to come and share a final strupak when they could tidy their minds of any lurking uncertainties and also check that their arrangements for the morning were fully understood.

She said as Isabel was leaving, 'Since Meggy is not here I shall take the late night tea and biscuits to the guests, but after that I shall go to my bed. It is unusual for any of the guests to stay out late on a Sunday night, but in case that should happen I take it you will be back to attend to them?'

'What's likely to keep anyone out late on a Sunday night?' scoffed Isabel.

After Kirsty had heard the couple leave she brewed another pot of tea, put out a plate of fresh-baked scones and went to the Smoking Room expecting to find Ruari. Much to her surprise he was not there. Since he'd mentioned earlier that morning that he was not intending to go to church she thought he might have gone up to his room for a quiet hour away from the other guests. She went upstairs and tapped lightly on his door and when there was no response she cautiously opened the door and peeped in. There was no one there. For a few moments she stood eyeing the room critically. Where was he? Even if he'd changed his mind and gone to church he should have been back by now. There would be no shops open to tempt him to linger; no other attractions to delay him, so where on earth would a God-fearing Islesman have got to on a gloomy Sunday afternoon, she asked herself, experiencing a flutter of trepidation as a succession of possibilities raced through her mind. What would happen if . . . ? With a determined shrug she closed the bedroom door and went back to the kitchen to carry on with her baking.

He came into the hall as she was setting out the Sunday evening meal in the dining room.

'I was looking out for you,' she whispered. 'I was wanting to speak to you for a wee whiley of somethings. Maybe over a strupak.'

He smiled regretfully. 'Can we not meet in the kitchen after the meal?' he suggested.

'No,' she told him. 'Isabel and her husband will be back soon and they will be in and out of the kitchen until they themselves go to bed. Sundays are always the same.'

'If I had known,' he began, but she cut him short. 'I myself did not know they were going out until it was too late to tell you,' she pointed out. 'I thought you would be spending the afternoon reading the Sunday papers but when I looked for you I couldn't find you.' He was looking disconsolate so she lightened her tone. 'Where on earth were you all this time anyway?' she teased him.

'Ach it was like this,' he began. 'You see my brother told me to get him a supply of tobacco for his pipe while I was in the city, and it was not until this morning that it came to my mind. When I spoke of it to one of the guests here he told me where was a tobacconist's shop that was open on Sundays so I hurried off there after dinner, not wanting to let my brother know I had forgotten to do what he had asked me.'

71

'It must have been a good distance away to keep you out so long,' she commented.

'No, indeed. It was not so far at all, but on the way back there was a band playing so I had a listen to it. They were good, too. I enjoyed it so much I didn't feel the time passing. I've a mind someone told me it was a kind of Salvation Band and when they came to me shaking their collection bags I put in a whole pound and I was pleased to do it.' Noticing her widening eyes he added, 'But I'm not so pleased that I missed our strupak.'

The mention of the band playing reminded her to speak to him about her wireless set. He frowned. 'I doubt there would be any use for it on Westisle,' he said. 'But perhaps you should bring it and very likely my brother is good enough with his fingers to get it sorted for you. Wireless is not such a great mystery to him as it is to me.' After a moment's thought he said, 'My brother has a gramophone and plenty of records which he will no doubt be willing to play for you.'

At the mention of his brother she experienced a slight sense of shock and realised that she had been so preoccupied with her own problems, her own doubts and questions, that the knowledge that she would be sharing a house not only with her new husband but with her husband's brother, had impinged only fleetingly on her thoughts. She had not entirely forgotten he would be one of the household but she had somehow disconnected him from her mental pictures of what life would be like in her new home.

Ruari had portrayed his brother – the other Ruari – as being bigger and stronger than himself, as a fine fisherman, a hard-working shepherd, a scholar and a competent handyman, and until he'd spoken of him as being the owner of a gramophone and many records and as perhaps having the skill to 'sort' a modern thing like a wireless set she'd seen him as very much an outdoors man, probably coming into the house only to eat and sleep. In fact as a hazy, undemanding figure moving in the background. But a gramophone was hardly an outdoor amusement, she reminded herself, and being 'good with his fingers' did not fit the description of a hard-working crofter fisherman. It seemed she would have to reassess Ruari Mhor when she met him.

'Will I pack your wireless in my portmanteau?' Ruari asked.

'If you think it will be safe in there,' she agreed. 'I'm afraid there is not enough room in mine.' She glanced at the clock. 'I must brew the tea and put the food on the tables,' she told him. 'It is only kippers and bread and butter tonight,' she added with a hint of apology.

'Is it *Oidhche Mhath*, till the morning then?' he queried a little wistfully.

'It must be so.' He stood by the table, looking as if he wanted to say something more but she pressed her hand on his shoulder. 'Sit you down now, ready to enjoy your kippers,' she bade him with a smile. 'The rest will be here in a minute and will not be pleased if I am late with their food.'

Before she got into bed that night she took her wedding ring from the matchbox in which she had secreted it on her wedding day, and put it on her finger. Already she felt a different woman.

Kirsty set her alarm clock to go off an hour earlier the next morning, and when it woke her she was surprised but relieved to find that instead of the restless night she had expected, she had enjoyed a good six hours sleep. Slipping into her morning dress she crept down to the kitchen and started preparing breakfast for guests.

While the porridge was simmering she quietly laid the tables in the dining room and then, returning to the kitchen, buttered what she considered to be an ample supply of scones and wrapped them in greaseproof paper. She then hardboiled half a dozen eggs and finally, filled her thermos flask with freshly brewed tea. They would not go hungry on their journey, she resolved and since she could not imagine Isabel would offer to pay her due wage for the past month she felt no compunction about helping herself to a reasonable quantity of food.

After the guests had left the dining room she swiftly cleared the tables, washed the dishes and stoked the range, then, satisfied that she had left everything as it should be she went back to her room and packed her nightclothes and her morning dress before changing into the clothes she was to wear for travelling. At the door of her room she paused for a minute or so as if to imprint it on her memory. It was a dingy little room but for so long she had been content to nestle in its dinginess that the moment of leaving it, knowing she would never again seek its sanctuary, caused an unlooked-for throb of emotion.

Leaving the door wide open for Ruari to collect her portmanteau and take it down to the vestibule ready for the taxi, she started down the stairs. When she was half-way down Isabel came out of the Smoking Room flourishing a duster. She stood looking at Kirsty with cold questioning eyes. Kirsty braced herself for the encounter as she descended the last few steps.

'Where'd you think you're off to, all dressed up at this hour of the morning?' Isabel accosted her.

Kirsty managed to swallow the dry lump that had formed in her throat. 'I am going to the railway station,' she said with dignity.

Isabel's mouth dropped open. 'You're *what*?'

'I am going to the railway station,' Kirsty repeated. 'I am leaving ISLAY and I am leaving my job here,' she elucidated.

Isabel appeared momentarily dumbstruck. Her mouth opened and closed but no sound came; her body seemed first to crumple and then to stiffen as, arms akimbo, she glared at Kirsty with eyes that looked to be in danger of popping out of their sockets. 'You can't do that,' she managed to screech. 'You can't leave without giving me due notice. It's the law. You just go and take off your coat and get back into that kitchen!' she commanded, her voice seeming to reverberate around the hall.

Nonchalantly Kirsty changed her handbag from one arm to the other while she regarded Isabel with an inscrutable smile. She waited, sensing Isabel would have a lot more to say as soon as she could regain control of her breathing. She did. 'If Mac was here he'd soon tell you what he thinks of you,' she stormed. 'He's always said you're a deceitful wretch of a woman and now I know he was right.'

Kirsty's smile widened. 'Mac's opinion of me would not make the slightest difference to my intentions,' she said. 'I won't waste my breath telling you my opinion of him.'

'Well I'm telling you, me and Mac have provided a good job and a good home for you here. You've had an easy enough life and anyone would think you'd show a bit of gratitude instead of leaving me without warning to cope on my own.' Her mouth twisted scornfully. 'You may as well know I've already got someone who will be willing to replace you,' she taunted.

'I guessed so,' Kirsty observed quietly.

Through the glass panel of the vestibule door she saw Ruari busying himself in the porch and realised the taxi had arrived. Not wanting Isabel to see that she was to share the taxi she moved so as to screen the panel from Isabel's view and at the same time to deter an anxious Ruari from entering too suddenly.

She held out her hand. 'Goodbye then, Isabel. Let there be no more recriminations.'

Isabel looked disdainfully at Kirsty's proffered hand. 'If you are holding out that hand for wages,' she said, her eyes narrowing spitefully, 'you're not getting any.' Kirsty winced as she swiftly withdrew her hand. With a haughty rasp of dismissal Isabel rushed into the kitchen and slammed the door.

At that moment Ruari came to bring down her portmanteau and take it into the vestibule. Kirsty watched him silently and then, with a sigh of relief that the confrontation with Isabel had been less wounding than she had prepared herself for, she gave one fleeting glance around *ISLAY*'s so familiar hallway before going confidently to the waiting taxi to join her husband for the first stage of their journey to Westisle.

Their train was not scheduled to leave for another hour, but they were told that it was already waiting at the station. The ticket collector advised them to take their seats as soon as possible, to make sure they would be comfortable so, finding a compartment in which two window seats were unoccupied they settled themselves for the journey. Ruari had bought a newspaper and Kirsty had bought a woman's magazine, more because she thought it looked the right thing to do rather than expecting it to provide a source of interest for the journey. While the train remained stationary she perused the magazine abstractedly, but with the first puff of the engine as it steamed out of the station excitement began to throb through her. She put the magazine in her handbag.

Nearly thirty years had passed since she had made that first train journey from her Granny's home to the city, and then she'd been too stunned by the eventualities that had brought such an abrupt change in her young life, and too overawed at finding herself actually travelling in anything so spellbindingly improbable as a train that she had retained only the sketchiest memories of the journey.

Now, since Ruari had discarded his paper and seemed inclined to sleep while the rest of the passengers were happy to ignore her she willingly allowed herself to be captivated, during the remaining hours of daylight, by the ever-changing scenery through which the train raced, and when night fell there was hardly less enjoyment in glimpsing the lights of distant towns and cities which emerged from the darkness only to be speedily enfolded by it. She was so absorbed by all there was to see that she hardly noticed the discomfort of sitting upright all night but she became aware of her cramped limbs when, shortly after a laggard dawn, they had to scurry through heavy rain to change to another train.

They were fortunate enough to have a compartment to themselves on the second train and since they were able to make themselves more comfortable Kirsty was not unduly dismayed that the rain obscured the scenery. She closed her eyes and it seemed no time at all before the train was slowing and with a long piercing whistle, announcing its impending arrival at their station. She roused Ruari and made herself ready to leave the train. 'This will be our station, will it not?' she enquired.

He nodded affirmatively and lifted their luggage down from the rack. 'I'm thinking the weather is looking kind of coarse,' he said, wiping the window and peering through the rain.

'The day doesn't seem to have got any lighter,' she commented.

The train jolted to a stop at a windblown platform where a solitary porter stared at it sourly as if resenting its presence there. Ruari unloaded the cases and carried them to an ancient-looking conveyance which he referred to as 'the bus'. Kirsty stepped down on to the platform to face a biting wind that brought the sharp fresh, instantly-remembered smell of the sea. She wanted to inhale deeply but the wind was too chilly. She looked at Ruari. 'What now?' she enquired.

'Ach, we have a wee way to go on the bus just,' he explained.

There were only two other passengers and they dismounted after a couple of miles. Buffeted by wind and lashed by the heavy rain the bus juddered its way along a deviating track across the rapidly darkening moors. It eventually pulled to a stop beside an entrance to a croft-house which Ruari described as the Post Office. Here Ruari and the bus driver began a discussion in Gaelic from which Kirsty was able to gather that the weather was too wild for a boat to cross to Westisle that night. Her heart sank. She was cold and she was tired and she was hungry, despite the hard-boiled eggs and scones they had consumed on the journey. Forlornly she looked out but it was too dark now to see the sea, let alone the Island which was to be her home. Turning away from the driver Ruari spoke to her.

'I will go now and have a word with Mairi Jane,' he said. 'She will know what to do.'

Making for the door of the crofthouse he opened it, and after shouting an enquiry disappeared into the lamplit interior. A few minutes later he reappeared followed by a small woman who was carrying a hurricane lamp and talking animatedly. The woman whom Kirsty guessed was Mairi Jane climbed on to the bus.

'Well, *mho ghaoil, Ciamera a Tha,*' she greeted Kirsty. 'This is indeed a surprise for us, is it not? But many a welcome you'll have. It is good to hear that Ruari has taken a wife.' Her welcome was warm yet not effusive; her broad smile was genuine and her handshake firm. Kirsty immediately took a liking to her.

Mairi Jane turned to the bus driver. 'And what have you to say to Ruari's new wife?' she asked him.

The man, who was in the act of taking a dram from the bottle of whisky Ruari had offered him, wiped the back of his hand across his mouth before shaking Kirsty's hand. 'It is good to welcome a new face,' he said and added uncertainly, 'Surely Westisle will be the better of a woman.'

'And she has the Gaelic!' Mairi Jane announced, much in the same way a chorus girl might announce she was to marry a millionaire. The bus driver smiled his approval.

Ruari interposed, 'Mairi Jane has kindly said she will give you a bed for the night until the storm quietens. I myself will go and have a word on Padruig and see what he thinks of the weather. He is a good judge and he is a good boat man.'

'Is it kind?' chuckled Mairi Jane. 'Surely I will give you a bed for the night and be glad of your company. Indeed, it's welcome you'll be to my house.' She turned to Ruari. 'You will take your luggage into the house now and Kirsty your wife will come with me, seeing I have the lamp,' she directed.

Kirsty, feeling she had been temporarily assigned to Mairi Jane, murmured grateful acknowledgements and followed her into the house where there was an ample peat fire above which a large black kettle swung. Waiting snugly on the hob stood a shiny brown teapot. It all looked so familiar she could almost imagine her Granny occupying the empty chair beside the range.

'Now, Bheinn Ruari, we will take a lamp to the bedroom up the stairs and then you will see if it pleases you,' Mairi Jane said. Lighting another lamp she led the way up a short flight of narrow stairs and, opening the door of a bedroom placed the lamp on a table beside the already made-up bed. 'There now!' she said, stepping aside to await Kirsty's comments.

To Kirsty the room seemed to have a 'ready and waiting' air about it. The bed appeared invitingly cosy; the sheepskins on the floor looked freshly washed and combed; the chest of drawers and the mirrored dressing table were surprisingly modern for a crofthouse and the lamplight reflected the care which had been patently lavished on it.

'My, but it surely invites one to sleep in it,' Kirsty exclaimed heartily. 'I believe I could throw myself into the bed and not wake until the day after tomorrow.'

'Then if you are satisfied I will take this hot water bottle out of the bed,' Mairi Jane reached under the bedcoverings and drew out a hot water bottle, 'and I will hot it up ready for when you wish to go to bed. It will keep you warm maybe until your man gets back to warm you.'

She slanted a waggish glance at Kirsty before going on. 'See, I reckon to have the room ready for any passing visitor who's in need of a bed and a bite to eat, so I put in a hot water bottle every day to keep the bed sweet and dry. It is a good step either way to a hotel,' she explained. Closing the bedroom door, she said, 'Come now and you will surely be glad of a warm drink and a bite to eat. Ruari will no doubt be taking a strupak with Padruig.'

While she enjoyed the hot tea and scones and slices of dumpling that were offered, Kirsty tried to probe Mairi Jane's opinion of the two Ruaris and about the style of life she must expect on Westisle.

'It is a bonny Island right enough,' Mairi Jane said, 'but an Island life is not what I would wish for myself. Even with three or four families as there once were on Westisle the women had found it lonely. They had no school for the bairns and only a wee shed for them to gather on the Sabbath.' Mairi Jane shook her head sadly. 'Not one of the women cared to go back, not even for a gift of three cows and twenty sheep would they consider it.'

'From what I've learned the two brothers are happy enough there.'

'Happy enough certainly, I'd say. They're good fishermen and good workers both and neither of them wanting in sense. Whether Ruari Mhor will be the happier for having a woman in the house I wouldn't know. He's a dour man and will not be easily parted from his work or from his books. But folks speak well of him as they do of Ruari Beag. You couldn't wish for a better husband and you will be sure of having a good home.'

'Well, hopefully this storm will be quieter by morning and I shall be able to cross and see my new home for myself.'

'Surely the storm will have quietened,' Mairi Jane comforted her. 'And surely that cattle man will be here ready for the sale.' Her voice was tinged with disdain. Kirsty looked at her with raised eyebrows.

'Is he not one for giving fair prices for your cattle?' she asked.

'There's some say he does and some say he doesn't,' Mairi Jane told her. 'I myself cannot say since I no longer have cattle.'

'He has favourites?' Kirsty thought it might prove useful to gather the information.

'He has plenty of money for favourites,' said Mairi Jane. 'And doesn't he come over here – a big man and all acock – with a voice that near deafens the head off one and he has his wee clerk beside him carrying a poc stuffed tight with notes. And I'm after hearing that any woman who has a beast or two for sale, poor as they may look, she'll likely get a good price for them from him. Maybe not at the sale but afterwards, when there's no menfolk around. And it's not unknown for him to give her a calf to rear for him, promising he'll pay her a good price for it at the next sale.' Mairi Jane sniffed. 'More fools them,' she disparaged, 'seeing the calves he leaves may not have the right number of legs.'

Kirsty stifled a yawn. 'I think I'll not wait up for Ruari,' she said. 'If you don't mind I'll take my hot water bottle and go to my bed.'

'Indeed,' Mairi Jane agreed. 'It's likely to be an early start for you in the morning if the sea settles itself for a whiley.'

It was barely daylight when Kirsty heard Ruari calling her to make herself ready for the boat. She rose and dressed quickly and found him waiting impatiently in the kitchen. 'My brother is here with the boat,' he told her, 'and he is anxious to go back and collect the cattle and ferry them across here for the sale while the tide is right and the sea is calm. It's more than likely it will blow up again by the evening.'

Mairi Jane appeared, hastily pushing her hair beneath an old black beret. 'My! Are you for away?' she exclaimed.

'We are so, and no time to spare,' Ruari responded.

'Ach, and here's me thinking I would have a good breakfast ready for you before you left,' she lamented. 'Can you not wait to take a wee cup in your hand just,' she pressed.

'No, no,' Ruari refused, brusquely picking up the two

portmanteaux and striding in the direction of a rough slipway where a small boat was moored.

Kirsty had time only to say a hasty farewell to Mairi Jane before hurrying after her husband. She could see there were two men standing on the slip beside the boat and she wondered which of them was her brother-in-law. She peered at them, trying to detect some likeness but the damp wind filmed her eyes and made her peering useless.

As Ruari approached the boat one of the men leapt down ready to take the cases. The second man remained where he was and watched. He paid no attention to Kirsty and for a moment or two she was uncertain of what to do. In the city she'd grown used to ignoring strangers but now she was back in the Islands she must shed city ways.

She managed an irresolute smile as she called out '*Tha e Breagha!*'

In acknowledgement the man grunted a barely audible '*He Breeah!*' at the same time indicating that she should get abroad and seat herself on the middle thwart. He offered no help as she gingerly lowered herself over the gunwale and sat on the middle thwart facing the bow.

As soon as the cases were satisfactorily stowed Ruari started to root in the cubby-hole and produced an old oilskin which he tied over them. His companion stepped quickly over the thwarts to reach the stern and after a shouted leave-taking the man on the slip untied the mooring rope and threw it to Ruari: the next moment the boat was chugging towards a lone wedge-shaped Island which, with a gesture, Ruari pointed out as Westisle. She tried to hold Ruari's eye but he had turned again to the bow. She guessed he would prefer to occupy himself there, no matter how unimportant the task, rather than come and sit beside her and since she wanted him to confirm only that it was his brother Ruari Mhor in the stern she chose not to embarrass him. It hadn't surprised Kirsty that he had not attempted to introduce her. She was well accustomed to being disregarded and in any case, a small

83

boat riding a choppy sea was hardly the place to exchange handshakes, she told herself.

She settled herself to renew her acquaintance with the sea, contentedly listening to the breaking of the bow-wave and the slap of the sea against the boat's sides and it came to her gradually that through all the years she had spent in the city, the image of the sea in all its moods had remained ineradicably in her mind; just as the sound of it had been a subdued melody in her ears.

On an impulse she tilted her chin to catch a splash of the flying spray on her face and the next moment her tammy was blown from her head. 'Oh!' she cried despairingly, twisting herself round on the thwart to see if there was any chance of retrieving it but her hair, blowing across her face, obscured her vision.

There was a sharp shout from the stern and, clawing her hair away from her face, she was able to glimpse clearly the man she assumed must be her brother-in-law. He was holding the tammy out to her but as she was about to try and crawl towards him her husband pushed her aside and snatched the tammy from his brother's grasp. She looked up at her brother-in-law and smiled gratefully, but her smile died as she saw his hard set jaw and his impassive eyes instantly dismissing her from his line of vision. Stung, she again turned to face the bow and, replacing her tammy, tied it on with her scarf.

As they neared the Island she could make out the pattern of boulders that marked a cleared channel where a small boat might nose in. The engine slowed; Ruari took the mooring rope and leaped ashore. His brother darted forward, swiftly lifted the cases on to a boulder that was still being splashed by the sea, and as swiftly darted back again to the stern. Kirsty rose from her seat.

'Are you ready?' Ruari called and when she nodded to him he offered a helping hand. The boulders were slimy and fearing she might lose her foothold, she gripped his arm tightly. His own grasp of her hand did not tighten and again she attributed it to embarrassment because of his brother's presence. As soon as they'd reached the short dry sward Ruari went back for the cases which he carried up and set beside her. There was a shout from the boat.

'I must away,' Ruari said. 'We have to get the cattle float from the far side of the Island before the tide goes back any further.'

Kirsty listened to him open-mouthed. 'But where's the house?' she demanded. 'You're surely not expecting me to wait here until you get back?'

'No, no, indeed. You'll find the house at the back of the wee brae there just. My brother says he has left a good fire and there are plenty of peats handy. You will make yourself comfortable until we get back from the sale.' She stared at him with a kind of amused disbelief. There was another shout from the boat. 'I'm away,' he insisted, hurrying down to the boat. 'You will find everything you want. *Oidhche Mhath* till this evening,' he called.

She stood there watching the boat being manoeuvred away from the boulder-strewn shore. Ruari waved an arm as they speared off out of sight beyond a sgurr of rock that stretched out from the land like a withered arm. Now what do I do? she asked herself. Leaving the cases to look after themselves she braced herself to go in search of the house. 'At the back of the wee brae' Ruari had instructed her and true enough when she had negotiated a short steep path she saw the house nestling in the glen below.

Her heart bounded at the sight of it. It was a grand-looking house to be a crofthouse. Even grander than she had envisaged from Ruari's description. And this was to be her home! An incredulous smile spread slowly over her face and, leaning against a convenient boulder beside the path, she paused and allowed herself to appraise the house more fully. As her hurrying heart steadied she became aware with breathcatching satisfaction that the smell of peat smoke drifting in the wind seemed to be offering its own welcome.

More eagerly now she carried on until she had reached

the end of the path, crossed an area of grass which evidently had been kept well-scythed and then on to a cobbled path alongside the house. Although she felt sure there would be no one there she approached the house timidly, uncertain as to whether she should simply lift the latch and enter or whether she should call out first. She compromised by giving a series of loud coughs before she pushed open the door. Once inside she again reassured herself by shouting, 'There is no one here, is there?' The lack of response was heartening and she ventured as far as the threshold of what she perceived through the half-open door to be a well-used living room. She sniffed. What degree of cleanliness could one expect two bachelor brothers to have maintained, she wondered, but she could smell nothing but the familiar peat reek. Nervously she entered the room. It was drab but it looked austerely clean. The wood-lined walls were stained dark with peat smoke; the linoleum that covered the floor was dun-coloured with wear but it was well swept. The sturdy furniture, the waxcloth covered table, the long low bench beneath the window, and the two armchairs either side of the range all proclaimed they had been fashioned from driftwood. The range itself, though not burnished as a woman might have kept it was not, in Kirsty's opinion, discreditably lustreless. The grate was piled with damp peats from which a tiny tendril of blue smoke curled fitfully while a couple of black iron kettles stood on the hob and a smoke-smudged metal teapot waited on a trivet beside the hearth. There was such an air of familiarity about it that she knew she had only to reach up to the mantelpiece to find the tea caddy.

Taking off her outdoor clothes she hung them on a hook which, as she expected, was on the door and then sitting down in one of the armchairs she considered her circumstances. She did not resent being left alone. Tides and storms she well knew governed Island life and cattle sales were too infrequent to be dismissed lightly. A beast ready for sale might show no profit if kept back until the next sale. She'd grown up with that knowledge, and despite her years in the city the knowledge had remained rooted in her memory. But coping alone in a strange and empty house on a strange Island she found intimidating.

She shivered. The room was not very warm and rising, she took a layer of the damp peats from the top of the fire and poked in some dry ones just as she had seen her Granny do and after a few puffs from a pair of bellows that hung beside the range the peats were soon glowing red. She smiled reminiscently as memories which had grown frail reasserted themselves. It took only a few minutes for the kettle to boil and only moments before she had a pot of tea brewing.

Searching for something to eat she lifted the lid off a large wooden barrel which stood by the wooden bench and was rewarded by the sight of a good poc of oatmeal on top of which lay two cloth-wrapped bundles, one enclosing girdle scones, the other oatcakes. Again she smiled. Her Granny had used an oatmeal barrel for just such a purpose.

Putting two scones on the table she replaced the rest in the barrel and then hunted around for a likely food store. A door, lower than the one through which she had entered, looked promising. In every other crofthouse she had seen, such a door would have opened on to nothing more than a recess bed but recalling that this house had been built by the Laird for his son it seemed likely that such a utility would be neither required nor planned. Opening the door she found herself in what she would have called a scullery. There was a sink graced by a single brass tap, a large cupboard with perforated zinc doors and a dresser, the shelves of which were not filled with crockery but with coloured glass netfloats and a miscellany of driftwood shapes and varied stones.

It was in a cupboard at the bottom of the dresser that she found the food she was looking for; butter, sugar, jam, flour, crowdie and a jug of milk. Two full bottles of whisky stood on one corner flanked by half a dozen mugs, a selection of whisky glasses, several bowls and a random assortment of cooking utensils. Taking what she needed back to the kitchen she drew a chair up to the table and buttered one of the scones. She bit into it warily and judged it not as good as one of her own but quite palatable. If this was a sample of her brother-in-law's cooking, she reckoned he would not prove to be much of a rival.

As she ate and drank she surveyed the room and planned how little she would have to do to make it more cheerful. Some bright curtains for the bare windows, the dresser brought out from the scullery and, after being given a coat of paint, enlivened by some colourful crockery. She would have to tread carefully; she must not be impatient nor must she demand change. But surely they would not be averse to a few small improvements, not even her dour brother-in-law. She rested her arms on the table and her head on her arms. Pictures formed in her mind of the kitchen as she would like it to be but the pictures were dispersed by the desire for sleep. Her head lay more heavily . . .

The room looked even more drab when she awoke and, horror-stricken, realised the light was beginning to fade. She glanced about her for a clock but no clock was visible. Somewhere at the back of the house she could hear the querulous cries of neglected hens. That was something she must do, she decided, and throwing her mac over her shoulders she raced outside towards a building which she'd identified as a barn. There as she expected she found an opened boll of corn with a tin measure resting on it. Filling the measure twice she threw the corn to the poultry and then investigated the other buildings to make sure they contained no other livestock which needed attention. They were all empty.

As she walked back to the house she could feel the strengthening wind tearing at her and, wondering if the brothers could have landed on the Island while she had been sleeping, she pulled her mac tightly around her and retraced her path to the clearing where she had come ashore that morning. The cases were still where Ruari had left them. She scanned the stretch of sea that separated Westisle from the mainland, hoping to glimpse the boat approaching but the increasing wind and the fading light made it impossible for her to discern anything smaller than a battleship, she reckoned.

She went back to the house pondering what she should do. Would they have had a meal after the cattle sale, she asked herself. Should she prepare a pan of soup? Resolving to see what food might be there she went into the scullery again and looked in the zinc-doored cupboard, where she found a skinned rabbit and a bowl of salt herring. There'd been a good store of potatoes in the barn, she recalled, so the best thing for her to do was to cook a pan of salt herring and potatoes and then if, when they returned the brothers had no appetite for such food, it would make good feed for the poultry.

She prepared the meal in the same way as she had seen her Granny prepare it – first stirring the unpeeled potatoes in a pail of water to clean the skins, then putting them into a large pan of water and topping them with a layer of salt herring. By then setting the pan on the hob to steam, her Granny had maintained, in the time it took the potatoes to cook, just the right amount of salt would have seeped from the fish to flavour the potatoes, also 'mildening' the herring, and her Granny's herring had always been good.

Replenishing the peat fire she set the pan on the hob and, after a glance through the salt-filmed window, went to the outer door and standing in its shelter, imbibed the distant roar of the sea and the noise of clean, wind-driven rain rustling in the bare branches of the rowan trees as it raced through the glen.

Going back into the kitchen she checked that the lamp was full of paraffin, lit it and placed it on the table. Its glow seemed to soften the austerity of the room and she sat by the fire letting her mind again form pictures of how she would like the room to be. Bright linoleum on the floor; cushions on the armchairs and on the bench; one or two pictures on the walls; a mirror perhaps? She went to the range and prodded the potatoes in the pan, and while she was doing so heard the unmistakable clumping of gumboots on the cobbled path outside.

Her husband, red-faced with sea and windburn, hailed her as he entered and began to shrug himself out of his oilskins. She looked at him with a gently enquiring smile and when she saw the sparkle in his eyes she suspected that a few drams of whisky had contributed to the colour of his face. Or maybe it was simply the result of good prices at the cattle sale, she excused him.

'My, my, but that pot smells good,' he said, coming towards her and boldly planting a kiss on her cheek. She flinched at the unexpected ardour of his greeting and darted a surreptitious glance at her brother-in-law to see if he showed signs of disapproval, but it appeared he had either not witnessed it or was not remotely interested. He was taking off his seaboots and when he had finished, he went over to the range and, taking one of the boiling kettles from the hob, went into the scullery, closing the door behind him.

Kirsty looked questioningly at her husband, who was helping himself to potatoes and fish from the pan. 'He is not pleased to see me?' she asked.

'Not yet just,' he admitted.

'Have you told him I am your wife?'

'I have so.'

'And what had he to say?'

'Only that I was foolish and we had no need of a woman here,' Ruari prevaricated. 'Ach, he will take to you before much time has passed,' he went on, in a tone too doubtful to be encouraging. 'He will be glad to have someone to cook for us and to see to the hens.'

'Oh, I did find corn and I fed the hens,' she told him. 'They seemed hungry so I hope I did right.'

'You did indeed do right,' he complimented her. 'And this fish and potatoes are greatly to my liking,' he added, licking at his fingers. His eyelids were drooping and his

90

voice was sleepy. 'We have brought up the portmanteaux,' he drawled.

'Ruari!' Kirsty said. 'You must show me tomorrow where I shall find the cows to milk, and tell me what other stock you have and how they are fed. All this I am willing to begin doing tomorrow as soon as it is light.' His head was beginning to nod and she went on urgently, 'But now you must show me the bedroom I am to sleep in. I have not yet had an opportunity to take a good look at the house and in any case, I thought you might not wish me to do so, but I need to know where is my bed.'

He roused himself. 'It is the door across the passage,' he told her. 'It is the room my parents used to sleep in and when they passed on it became my room.' His matter-of-factness disconcerted her.

'Show me,' she invited, and pulled him up from his chair.

The bedroom, like the kitchen was austerely clean and contained a double bed, two large chests of drawers and two brass-bound chests that looked as if they had once belonged to some seafarer. The bed was covered with blankets but there was no sign of sheets and the pillows were of plain ticking.

'She is a good bed,' her husband told her, in a slurred voice. 'And stuffed with feathers from our own birds.'

'She is not damp?' she questioned.

He looked at her, shocked. 'I have never wet a bed since I was a child,' he denied. 'And this mattress goes outside in the sun every spring.'

'No, no,' she hurried to say. 'I was meaning rain damp.' Her grin was apologetic. 'And you don't use sheets or pillowcases?' she asked.

'Not since my mother died I don't, but in one of the chests there you will find plenty of sheets and things packed away in bog myrtle. My mother always kept them that way.'

Kirsty was relieved. She hadn't fancied sleeping in blankets though she had been well-used to doing so when she was a child. 'I should like to put sheets and pillowcases on the bed before I sleep in it,' she told him. 'Can we sort them now?'

He lifted the lid of one of the brass-bound chests to reveal neatly folded piles of white linen. Kirsty lifted out a pair of sheets, a bolster case and two pillowcases, exclaiming delightedly as she pressed them to her face to detect the faint but still discernible fragrance of bog myrtle. While she was making the bed Ruari went back to the kitchen and when she returned he was fast asleep on his chair and snoring loudly.

'You'd best get to your bed, Ruari,' she told him severely and again grasped his arm in an effort to pull him out of his chair. He protested but was obviously in favour of going to bed and made no resistance when she put an arm around his shoulders and guided him to the bedroom. 'Now you will take off your jacket and trousers and get into your bed, Ruari,' she directed him. 'And I will come when I have dried my nightdress. I daresay it has got damp lying in the portmanteau.'

He grunted and sat down on the bed.

Kirsty returned to the kitchen and opened her portmanteau, took out a nightdress and draped it on a chair in front of the fire. She made herself a cup of hot milk and sat beside the range, moving her nightie from time to time to ensure that it was thoroughly dry. She was startled when the scullery door opened suddenly and her brother-in-law came into the room. Surreptitiously she watched him take a couple of scones from the barrel, butter them lavishly and, still holding them in his fist, leave the kitchen presumably to go to his bedroom. He'd made no acknowledgement of her presence. Indeed, for all the notice he'd taken of her the kitchen could have been quite empty. She wouldn't have been at all surprised if he'd douted the lamp before leaving the kitchen and left her in the dark.

After topping the fire with damp peats to keep it alight until the morning she picked up her nightie and carried the lamp through to the bedroom she was to share with her husband. She found his jacket and trousers had been just dropped on the floor while he himself lay slantwise across the bed. He made no murmur as she pushed him aside, rearranged the covering blankets and crept timorously into the bed beside him.

Kirsty thought she had slept only lightly, if at all, that night but when the night sky was beginning to be washed by a grey dawn she became conscious that she was alone in the bed in a quiet bedroom, a quiet house and, since she could hear no noise of wind, a quiet land. Evidently Ruari had managed to slip away in the early dawn during one of her fitful spells of slumber and what she had keyed herself up to expect to happen some time during the night had simply not happened. There had been no intimacy. She was still a virgin.

For a few minutes she lay examining her emotions, identifying a sense of relief mingled with an unaccountable sense of disappointment. She hadn't looked forward to intimacy but she had prepared herself to submit to it, and now she was experiencing an inexplicable sense of letdown. Was this marriage, she asked herself. Had he been too drunk? Or too shy? Was he impotent? Was he too much in awe of his brother's disapproval? On the other hand, was there something about her which, on closer acquaintance, had made her less attractive to him? She wondered how long it would be before the answers were forthcoming. Meantime she must be prepared to respond to him whenever he might approach her. And if he proved to be impotent, she reminded herself, it would make not the slightest difference to her. She had married him for a home and the ring on her finger.

It was still dark in the bedroom so she lit the lamp, dressed and went through to the kitchen. The glowing peats gave her a smug welcome, the kettle came to a swift boil and within a minute or two she had made a pot of tea and had a pan of porridge simmering on the hob. Since there were no used bowls on the table she assumed the two Ruaris had taken only a mug of thin brose before going about their morning chores: probably fishing, she deduced, since fishermen were known to favour the early hours.

After she'd eaten her own breakfast she finished unpacking the portmanteaux and not until then did she realise how unsuitable were her clothes for even the lightest landwork. She'd thought her old clothes would serve but inspecting them she could see how flimsy and inadequate they were for the conditions she would now have to face. She urgently needed to get herself a serviceable waterproof and a pair of gumboots. Last night she'd noticed a supply of oilskins hanging in a recess at the back of the passageway and a row of gumboots ranged below them. She looked to see if there were any there now and was relieved to find there were. Investigating them she found a pair of gumboots that were not too roomy to stay on her feet, and an oilskin that was not too voluminous to restrict her movements. Donning them she ventured out to feed the hens. They seemed surprised to be called to feed and she put it down to the earliness of the hour.

She scanned the weather prospects. The breeze, though it was no more than a breeze after the previous night's storm, was sharp and cold and run through with rain. Across the Sound she could see it teasing the hovering clouds to shred themselves on the gaunt dark hills of the mainland. The day would improve, she predicted.

The hens fed, she decided to do a little exploration of the Island and, going through a cattle gate, found herself on rough moorland that was scored with meandering sheep tracks, jumbled with craggy rocks and bounded this morning by heavy mist. Tramping placidly along the varying tracks and skirting the most formidable outcrops of rock, she began to congratulate herself on her recall of a terrain that struck her as being almost a replica of that she had been used to roaming barefoot in her childhood. Suddenly, one gumbooted foot squelched deep into a patch of sphagnum moss, causing her to step back quickly. She blamed herself that her native caution seemed to have deserted her momentarily. She ought to have remembered that treacherous bogs often concealed themselves beneath a coat of innocent-looking sphagnum.

She stood for a minute or two, estimating the likely extent of the bog and its possible depth, and decided that one of the first things she must do was to ask Ruari to accompany her on a reconnaissance tour of the Island and point out any similar hazards. Turning, she retraced her path to the house. Her over-large gumboots were tiring to walk in and years of pavement walking seemed to have devitalized not only her desire for exercise but also her stamina. She'd take herself in hand, she vowed. In no time at all she would be ranging over these moors, perhaps not barefoot and sadly not as lissomely, but with at least a good share of the energy she'd had in her earlier years.

When she got back to the house she found the two brothers just finishing their bowls of porridge. Her husband looked at her enquiringly.

'I've been doing a little exploration,' she explained, 'so I borrowed an oilskin and some gumboots. I hope that's all right?' She lifted her feet and the boots slid off. 'It is the first time I have ever worn gumboots, or boots of any kind to wander the moors. I had footwear only for going to church; the rest of the time I went barefoot.'

Ruari said, 'If you will tell me the size of your feet I will get you a pair from the store next time we are across.' He frowned. 'As for oilskins, I doubt they make such things for women but only for men just.'

'If you bring me the smallest men's size it should be suitable,' she told him. 'I believe I could cut some off if it was too long.'

He nodded agreement. 'I'm after thinking you've fed the hens,' he observed.

'I thought you would be wanting me to do that,' she said. 'I was always told that the earlier hens were fed the more eggs they would lay.'

'Maybe so,' he acknowledged, 'but when we need to go

early to catch the tide it is likely to be too early for the hens to be fed so they have to wait until we get back. We feed them once a day just and we find they lay well enough on that. Is that not so, Ruari Mhor?' he addressed his brother but there appeared to be no recognition from Ruari Mhor that he had been spoken to. He rose from the table, gathered up the two empty porridge bowls and went through to the scullery.

'I was trying to do what I thought was right,' Kirsty said. 'I well remember the morning and evening feeding of the hens was a kind of ritual in my Granny's time.'

'You can certainly bring them round to being fed twice a day if that's what would best please you,' he allowed. He grinned. 'No doubt they will be better for the pot that way.'

'If you will put me in mind of what you would like me to do then, just as I told you when we spoke of such things at ISLAY, when I promised to do my best to help you. I mind you mentioned there were cows to be milked but I've seen no sign of cattle hereabouts nor even when I was out on the moors.'

'It is only the one beast we milk,' he told her. 'The rest of the cattle have their calves running with them. They have the Island to roam just as the sheep.'

'And where is the milk cow?'

'She follows the rest of the cattle along with her calf, seeing we don't use much in the way of milk. All I do is when I go to feed them I take what milk the calf has left. She's a good milker, that particular cow, but if you will be wanting more milk you can bring her calf into the shed at night and then milk the cow before he gets to run with her again.'

'I don't suppose my small consumption of milk will make that necessary,' she assured him. 'But Ruari,' she hurried on, 'as soon as you can find the time, will you come with me for a good look at the Island so I can get my bearings and you can acquaint me with any hazards?

97

I'm asking you because I stepped into a bog this morning without seeing it was there at all.'

'Ach!' he said disdainfully. 'There are no bogs deeper than your knees on the Island. Indeed, there is nothing for you to be feared of at all. Unless,' he looked at her with a teasing expression. 'Unless,' he resumed, 'you will be feared of the wee folk.'

'Not specially,' she countered. 'Are you telling me there are still wee folk on Westisle? Have you met any?' she chaffed.

'The old folk believed there to be wee folk still here. They believed too that they had put a spell on Loch Mor so no beast would ever take a drink from it.'

'Are there other lochans on Westisle?' she asked him. 'I didn't see any this morning.'

'Just three and maybe one or two that can only be called lochans for a wee whiley after long rain. Westisle is a larger Island than it looks from the mainland and you will do a fair amount of roaming before you see the whole of it.'

'Is Loch Mor this side of the Island?' she pursued. 'I mean the one supposed to have the spell on it?'

'Ach, no. It is more in the middle of the Island where the land is low and where the storms are not as savage as they can be here.' He glanced at the salt-frosted window and then went on, 'I'll tell you, *Mho ghaoil*, what we'd best do now is to take the day's hay to the cattle and you will see which cow is to be milked. This way I shall be able to point out to you the different places they are likely to seek shelter in the different winds. After last night's storm I reckon they would have made for Glen Roag or else Camus beg. We shall find them some place, and as we look you will learn your way about the Island.'

'Right,' she agreed. 'When do you want to start off?'

'As soon as you have taken your strupak,' he said. 'There is still tea in the pot if that will suit you.'

'Is there nothing we should see to before we leave?' she queried, pouring herself a mug of tea.

He shrugged his shoulders. 'Nothing that I see. Ruari Mhor will clean the dishes before he goes off to his sleep and we shall be back in plenty of time to do whatever else must be done.' He put on his cap. 'I will away now and get the hay for the cattle and you will bring the milk pail that hangs beside the sink.'

Slipping on the borrowed gumboots once more and pulling on the oilskin she went outside. Ruari was coming away from the barn, a sack stuffed tight with hay tied across his shoulders, a stout crook in one hand and a small, what she had been used to calling a 'tinker pail' in the other. He handed her the pail, explaining that it contained a mash of oatmeal and herring bree which the milk cow was given as a supplement, bidding her at the same time to be sure to remember to do likewise when she went alone to do the milking, for fear the cow would not let her near without it.

The breeze was no longer laced with rain and there were even errant shafts of sunshine as they plodded on, she scrambling up rocky outcrops which he could take in a couple of strides and pausing more often than she cared to admit so as to slow her racing breath before hurrying to catch up with him. He did not notice or he politely ignored her occasional breathlessness, and strode on effortlessly while at the same time calling her attention to salient features of the terrain.

When they gained a view of a lochan, bleak and serene in a deep glen tended by a tangle of slim birch trees, she called to him to ask if this was the lochan which the wee folk had put a spell on so no cattle would drink from it. It was as much a pretext for getting him to pause for a few minutes as to hear about the lochan.

'It is indeed,' he told her. 'The old folk used to speak of it as the Glen of the Wee Folk but my mother always spoke of this place as the Glen of Bluebells. It is a rare sight in the spring when there is a breeze from the sea racing up the glen, bowing the bluebells and fairly carrying the scent of them across the Island.'

'Have you ever tasted the water of the lochan?' she enquired.

'I swallowed some only once, when me and my brother decided it would be a good place for us to learn to swim. I went in too deep and was trapped by the mud from my feet to my shoulders and my brother had to haul me out with a rope.' He grimaced. 'I got a good dose of the water then right enough and I've no wish to taste it again.'

He grinned. 'The pair of us got a good skelping that night for going near the lochan and we had to promise not to go there again.'

'But no ill-effects apart from the skelping?' she pursued.

'I lost a fair bit of my stomach that night but whether it was the lochan water or my father's skelping brought it on I never knew. I never risked going there again, seeing the bottom was that soft that if my brother hadn't hauled me out I believe I would have stayed there.'

'You were indeed lucky,' she commented.

They found the cattle near a shingle beach on the other side of the Island. 'Aye, I thought this was likely where they'd be,' Ruari said, making tracks towards them. Kirsty's heart warmed to them and she paused to take in a sight she had not witnessed since her childhood. There were seven cows, each with its calf and there was a magnificent bull. They were all true Highlanders, with black-ringed muzzles, handlebar horns and wind-combed coats, and when they saw Ruari they came eagerly but still decorously towards him. The bull was more leisurely in his approach. Was it because he was more gentlemanly or more timid, she wondered, suddenly remembering her Granny's staunch belief in the amiability of Highland bulls.

'Now can you still milk a cow, d'you think?' quipped Ruari. She turned on him with a challenging grin.

'Wait and see,' she retorted. He brought the cow to her and Kirsty squatted down. The beast was surprisingly docile and the calf was not too demanding to deny Kirsty the milk from two teats while it sucked the other two.

'There then,' she chuckled, standing up and showing him the contents of the pail. 'How's that for a start?'

He fed each cow a ration of hay from his bag and then led the way along an intricate pathway which brought them out above another shingle beach, where she could see a fishing boat and a cattle float moored a little way off the edge of the tide.

'These are your boats?'

'Indeed.'

She was surprised, and turned to him with raised eyebrows. 'But surely this beach is a good distance from the house, is it not?'

'Ah, but here is the best shelter on the Island and it is not far when you know it,' he refuted. 'There is a short cut that runs down the wee brae at the back of the house, so if we need to we can reach the boats in only a wee while.' He pointed along the beach. 'And there if you will look you will see a great boulder of rock and behind it the small boat is hauled up. It is safe there and it is very little trouble to drag it down to the water if it is needed.'

'Has it an outboard?' she asked.

'It has an outboard but I doubt you'll be able to manage it yourself,' he discouraged.

'And where is the Island that you go to for your peats?' she wanted to know.

He turned her to look north where a tiny, sea-misted Island lay like a crumpled discarded duster on the water.

'There,' he said. 'That is our peat Island. The hags there are black and deep and the peat is good for the fire. Here on Westisle as I told you there are peat hags but they are shallow and the peats are slow to boil a kettle.'

'It is certainly good solid peat you have in the stack by the house,' she agreed. 'And it burns almost as well as city coal.'

They were nearly back at the house before she thought to ask, 'Ruari, if I am to cook meals for you I need to know what food you like and what times you like to eat

101

it. I noticed at ISLAY that you seemed to enjoy the food I cooked but that was mostly cooked in an oven.'

'Me and my brother like the same sort of food, but mostly we eat fish and potatoes just. It is easy.'

'Will you be willing to try other kinds of food? I mean, things like pies and tarts and say, potatoes roasted instead of boiled?'

'Were those roasted potatoes you set beside the meat at ISLAY?' he asked.

'They were,' she confirmed.

'They were good. I fairly enjoyed them when I got used to them.'

'Would your brother be prepared to try such things?'

'I believe he would.'

'And things like tarts and pies baked in the oven?' She was feeling her way carefully.

'Aye,' he admitted.

'There's an oven in the range at the house isn't there? Do you know if it works?'

'It used to work for my mother,' he said.

'What sort of things did your mother cook in the oven?' she probed, desiring to please him.

'Oh, I mind she used to make a kind of gingerbread and a cod-liver loaf at times.'

'Not pies or pastry?'

He shook his head. 'We never ate such things in those days. We were satisfied to get scones and oatcakes and bannocks and a cloutie dumpling once or twice a year. That was the sort of food our father was best pleased with after he'd taken his soup or fish or rabbit. Was it not the same with yourself before you went to the city?'

'Indeed it was,' she agreed. 'There was an oven in the old range at my Granny's house but she claimed to have no knowledge of how to work it so it was never used. I don't believe it ever achieved a temperature higher than lukewarm no matter how many peats were piled on the fire. Apart from the girdle, I grew up with the idea that the only way to cook food was to boil it.'

102

'You soon got a taste for oven food when you went to the city?'

'Indeed I did. I got a taste for fruit, too. We'd not seen much fruit except for blaeberries and brambles and hazelnuts but they had such short seasons. My Granny wasn't one for making jam.'

'My mother made jam with the brambles and I'm saying it was good. There is good bramble picking on the Island here and blaeberries, too, in the summer. And there are nuts in the wood at the far end of the Island. We didn't go that far today but you will find them for yourself soon enough I doubt.'

'I'm surprised your brother didn't try making jam,' Kirsty said. 'He seems to have tried his hand at most things.'

'Ach, no. He couldn't be troubling himself with that sort of thing.'

'Well, as soon as the spring comes you will show me where the blaeberries are and the brambles and I shall certainly make jam,' she promised him. 'But when we get back to the house will you help me find out how the oven works?'

'Ach, my brother will show all that to you,' he demurred. 'I have never taken anything to do with it.'

'Your brother?' she exclaimed. 'He has not yet spoken to me nor shaken my hand nor noticed I am on the Island. He would never agree to show me how the oven works.'

'Ach, give him time just.'

'Your brother has no time to give me,' she retorted cynically. 'You will not ask him to show me how the oven works. I will find out for myself.'

That evening she again cooked what she had decided was a 'safe' meal of boiled fish and potatoes. To her it looked pallid and unappetising after her years of what was termed 'good plain cooking' such as she had been accustomed to serving at *ISLAY* but her first forkful renewed her acquaintance with fish, fresh-caught that day and with potatoes bursting from their skins light as whipped flummery. She ate with relish. Her brother-in-law came into the kitchen while she and Ruari were eating their meal but, though she had laid a place for him, he did not sit down at the table. Instead he picked up his plate, took it to the range, helped himself from the pans and then left the kitchen. He had not glanced at her and no word had been exchanged between the two brothers.

Despondently Kirsty looked at her husband. 'Don't let me come between you and your brother,' she entreated. ' I would far sooner go back to the city than I would let that happen.'

'You need have no fear of that,' Ruari replied. 'Though my brother is dour he is a good man. He will not turn against me nor I against him. Nor against you once he gets to know you,' he added.

'But I can't live here like an outcast,' she protested. 'That is how he makes me feel.'

'He will change towards you. It is with me he is a little angry. He thinks I have been foolish in bringing a woman here without first preparing for her arrival.'

'He could at least speak to me. For all the notice he takes of me I could be a ghost flitting about the kitchen,' Kirsty argued. 'Can't you explain to him that I expect nothing from him and I will keep out of his way as best I can?'

'In a wee whiley I will not need to explain anything,' he objected. 'I see already he is taking to you.'

With a heavy sigh she rose and began gathering up the dishes and the debris of the meal to take through to the scullery. Ruari made no offer to help her and when she returned to the kitchen he was sitting on the bench mending a lobster creel. She said, 'Ruari, did you notice the window is almost smothered in salt? Will you tell me what you use for cleaning the glass and where I am likely to find whatever it is?'

'I noticed it right enough, but it is too dark to clean windows, surely?' he ridiculed. 'You will not know whether the glass is clean or dirty until the birth of the morning.'

'No, I'm not daft enough to try cleaning windows in the dark,' she scolded him. 'But you will be going to your creels early in the morning so you will not be here to tell me where to look for things. Try and understand how strange this house is for me and how loth I would be to pry into what might be secret places.'

He dismissed her worries with a brief grunt of amusement. 'There are no secret places in this house,' he denied. 'Save for my brother's room, the house is open to anyone.'

'That big cupboard at the back of the passage,' she suggested. 'Am I likely to find cleaning things in that?'

'Indeed that is where you will find them but I doubt you will find any tool for cleaning windows since it is my brother who always cleans them.'

'I wouldn't expect to need a tool,' she reasoned. 'Just cloth dusters.' She'd had no experience of cleaning windows. Uncle Donny had simply thrown a pail or two of water over the windows at her Granny's cottage and in the city there'd been a regular window cleaner. But he hadn't used a tool!

'Ah, but my brother made himself a kind of tool that does the job better than any other thing,' he maintained.

She smiled sceptically. 'For all the use I'm likely to get of that I'd be best to try some wet cloths,' she said.

'Maybe he would be pleased to give you a lend of his tool,' Ruari suggested. 'Maybe he thinks cleaning windows is a woman's work.'

'I'll wait until he tells me so,' she said submissively. They chatted desultorily for a while until it became impossible for her to stifle her yawns. 'I am going to heat a mug of milk and take it to my bed,' she announced. 'I am gey tired.'

'You should take a dram of whisky with your milk,' he advised. 'It will help take some of the tiredness out of you.'

'I'm not sure I want the tiredness taking out of me

except by a good sleep,' she declared, and noticing his sudden crestfallen expression, she wondered if he had been disconcerted by what she had said.

Paying her no regard he went through to the scullery and returned with a half-empty bottle of whisky and two glasses. Just at that moment her brother-in-law entered the kitchen. Ruari looked enquiringly at his brother and then spoke to Kirsty. 'Kirsty, you will get another glass for my brother?'

'There is no need for another glass,' she replied. 'There are two glasses on the table and there are two people who want whisky, are there not?'

'But will you not be taking a dram yourself?'

'No, I will not.' She smiled as she shook her head emphatically. 'It is a long time since I have tasted the good rich milk of a Highland cow and I am not going to allow whisky to spoil it for me. You enjoy your whisky, I shall enjoy my milk,' she said. She thought her husband looked a trifle downcast as she picked up her mug of milk, bade him a warm 'Oidhche Mhath!' and went to the bedroom. She was asleep when he came to bed and roused herself only enough to be conscious of the distance between her body and his.

As on the previous morning Ruari rose early. Kirsty asked sleepily, 'Will I get up and make the porridge?'

'No, no,' he bade her. 'We will take a mug of brose just and be off to the creels. We will take our porridge when we get back. It's the way we're used to doing it.'

As soon as she heard them leave the house she got up and went into the lamplit kitchen where again she found the peat fire glowing red and the kettle steaming gently on the hob. She made tea and porridge, ate her own breakfast and then got out the girdle and baked some scones. It was still too dark to try cleaning the salt-caked window but she went to search for suitable cloths and cleaning materials in the big cupboard. She found some roughly-made dusters which she guessed had come from a tinker's bundle and which, since they were still neatly folded, she suspected had not yet made the acquaintance of dust. She also found a scrubbing brush and a floor mop which, unlike the dusters, looked well used. She was wrapping a batch of the cooled scones ready to put into the oatmeal bin when she heard seaboots clumping on the cobbles and then stamping into the house. Immediately she brewed a fresh pot of tea and moved the porridge pan a little nearer the fire.

'Good fishing?' she greeted her husband.

'No bad,' he replied. 'No bad at all.' From the tone of his voice she gathered the fishing had been pretty good. 'There's a few crabs in a pail out there and there's a lobster if you fancy such a thing,' he told her.

'I do indeed,' she said enthusiastically. 'There's nothing I like better than a lobster but the price of them in the city shops is so frightening I rarely tasted a claw. Will I cook it as part of your meal tonight?'

'Ach no,' he refused. 'Neither of us have a liking for lobsters though we don't say no to a crab or two.'

'But no,' she protested. 'You must not bring lobsters for me alone. It would be a waste of good money. I also like crabs cooked in the fire the way we talked of it at ISLAY. Is that the way you wish me to cook them when you are ready for your supper?'

'Aye so,' he approved.

'The tea is fresh brewed and the porridge is hot,' she advised him. 'I found cloths in the big cupboard as you said there would be and since there is light enough I will go and try to clean that window.' He made no comment as she went outside, where she found a pail which she filled from one of the big water butts at the end of the house. As she rubbed at the glass she could see the two men eating their porridge. Ruari Mhor seemed to approve since she saw him get up to take a second helping from the pan. Well, I've done something to his liking evidently, she gloated and rubbed a little harder at the window-pane.

Her efforts to clean the window met with little success. The salt was so adhesive she imagined it had been mixed with glue and though she rinsed and rinsed the cloths and rubbed and rubbed at the glass it looked as if she had been merely daubing it with salty smears. Exasperated she gave up. The water was creeping in chilly rivulets up the insides of her sleeves, her hands were stiffening with the cold and a sneaky breeze was harrying her legs. She emptied the pail and tucked her hands under her armpits to warm them. Thus, looking miserably hunched she went indoors.

Her husband glanced at her enquiringly.

'I cannot clean the salt off the window with these cloths,' she told him. 'And it is cold working outside for no result.'

'Ach, but the next rain will clean the window,' he encouraged.

'I doubt if rain will wash off the salt just,' she said morosely. 'It's that sticky you would think it has been

painted on with glue. I believe I will need to use a scrubbing brush when I try again.'

'Ach, but my brother knows the secret of cleaning the
salt off windows. Is that not true, Ruari Mhor?' He looked
eagerly at his brother.

There was a perceptible pause before his brother permitted the single monosyllable to escape his lips. 'Aye,'
he admitted.

'It's a kind of moss you gather, is it not?'

Again the pause. Again the monosyllabic 'Aye.'

'You will show Kirsty where you get it, or you will
bring some for her to try?'

A derisive twitch of his lips preceded Ruari Mhor's final
'Aye.'

Kirsty could feel the slight tension between the brothers
and went to the bedroom to change into a dry jersey.
When she got back to the kitchen her husband was again
wearing oilskins.

'You are away back to sea?' she questioned.

'We will be taking our lobsters to the salesman on the
mainland. Will there be messages you would wish me to
get there?'

'The things I spoke to you of,' she reminded him hesitantly, not sure if she should offer him payment. 'Gumboots and sou'wester and oilskins.'

'Indeed you will be needing such things and I'd already
planned to get them. Will I take a shoe to match the size?'

'No, no. I cannot spare a shoe. Just tell them I take
size five shoes so they had best send me size six gumboots
and I can then wear a couple of pairs of socks to fill them.'

'Is that the lot?'

'All I can mind. No doubt there will be a few groceries
I am needing but I will write a list for you to take with
you next time you are going to the mainland.'

He grunted an acknowledgement. 'I must away then,'
he said, hastily fastening his oilskins. 'My brother is
already down at the boat and he will not be best pleased
if I keep him back.'

'*Oidhche va*, then,' she called cheerily as she followed him outside. His reply was brusque and barely audible. He neither turned his head nor made any gesture of leave-taking.

Her mouth puckered into a rueful smile. Well, there you are Kirsty MacLennan, she reflected as she watched him striding away. You have got yourself a true Island man. Not a demonstrative man; not a city suitor and not by any means a gallant, but so long as he continues to behave kindly towards you, you must consider yourself a lucky woman. I will do my best to please him and to make his home the sort of place he will wish to return to. Indeed, she thought, the only difficulty that might stand in the way of their achieving at least a mildly affectionate relationship with one-another was her brother-in-law. Would he ever come round to accepting her presence in the household? Could she believe, as her husband encouraged her to believe, that it would not be long before her brother-in-law 'took to her'? How long would it be before he would even look at her, never mind speak to her, she asked herself. She must pray that time would indeed mellow his resentment, but until it did she must not permit herself to become either too pessimistic or too perturbed by his attitude.

Before going back to the house she fed the hens, stuffed a sack with hay for the cattle and made a potach for the milk cow. Then in the kitchen she took most of the hot peats off the fire, dropped them into a pail, carried it outside and left it on the cobblestones. This way, she reckoned, by the time she got back from the cattle the range would have cooled enough for her to easily locate the flues and dampers and perhaps to discover why the oven did not get hot.

Donning the oilskin and slipping her feet into the gum-boots she had worn the previous day, she set out to find the cattle. She was in no way overawed by the misty loneliness of the moors but rather felt that she was easing herself back into a childhood from which she had never managed to detach herself. How had she filled the intervening years? Had she been truly content? Had she really convinced herself that she'd known no yearning to go back to an Island life – that the city had claimed her? She knew this morning, as she drew in deep lungfuls of the sweet damp air, that the yearning had only lain dormant, that the moors were impatient to reclaim her. She felt an urge to kick off her gumboots and to walk barefoot through the moss and heather but she put the boots on again after a few steps. The moss was cold and wet and the heather was scratchy. When the warm weather came she must condition her feet to cope with it, she promised herself. She trudged on, her pleasure mounting as the morning brightened, the mist shredded itself into tendrils and the only sounds that broke the silence of the moors were the occasional bleatings of sheep, the mew of a buzzard and the clumping of her own gumboots.

She followed as nearly as she could recall the path which Ruari had shown her the previous day, stopping briefly to admire the 'spelled lochan' and the Glen of Bluebells where it was so still and quiet that even the trees seemed to be listening in the hope of detecting whispers of other life.

She found the cattle in much the same area as they had been the previous day, and when they saw her they raised their heads to look at her curiously but they did not approach. She started to pull hay from the sack and set it out in tufts and they began to come forward, apprehensively at first and then more trustingly. She was doubtful about being able to identify the milk cow but one of the herd disregarded the hay and came purposefully towards her. Kirsty offered the potach and crouched down to take her requirement of milk.

Instead of going back the way she had come, she decided to make her way across the Island and by so doing she came across a scattered settlement of derelict houses which she assumed had been the homes of the crofters who had abandoned the place so many years ago. Now sheep grazed on the short winter-crisped grass; rabbits scuttled among the moss-grown stones while a pair of hooded crows squabbled over a carcass. Resting on a boulder she contemplated the setting: the gentle slope down to the shingle shore where at that moment a stately heron was waiting at the edge of the tide for the sea to service him with a meal, while a couple of otters indulged in sinuous exploration of the dark sea-covered rocks. She thought, if I'd wanted to build a home this is the spot I would have chosen, not the place the Laird chose to build his son's house. Turning again to look at the ruined cottages she let her imagination people them with figures such as her Granny had described to her. Women, young and old, sitting at the doors of the cottages and working at their spinning wheels; men making nets or fashioning hazel withies into creels while children watched and learned; dogs lying in wait to chase a gull or a hooded crow which dared to venture too close to the dwellings.

She would have liked to linger there, but reminding herself of all the work she'd planned to do before the two men returned from the mainland, she started homeward.

The range was certainly cool by the time she got back and it was easy enough for her to locate the oven flues. One had jammed due to lack of use, but she managed to free it with the aid of an iron rod and a stone, and then with a long-handled scraper she had discovered in the barn, she began to take from under the oven shovelful after shovelful of tight-packed peat ash which she scattered on the turf at the back of the house, telling herself it would be good for the garden she planned to have there before very long. Next she gathered dry kindling and peats from the peat shed and lit the fire. It took off well and she very soon had a kettle boiling and a pot of tea brewing. Adjusting the dampers of the oven she piled peats on to the fire and after they had been glowing brightly for an hour or so she opened the oven door. Heat wafted out and she hastily shut the door again. It had been blocked with ancient peat ash and now she had found the flues she could make the oven hot whenever she wanted to. She was highly satisfied. She could experiment with dishes other than boiled fish and potatoes.

Estimating that it would be nearly dark again by the time the two brothers got back from the mainland, she made herself a strupak and sat meditating over what dish she could provide from the limited ingredients in the safe and which might appeal to both men. Apart from fish there was butter and milk; there were plenty of potatoes in the clamp in the barn; there was oatmeal and there was flour. There was a paunched rabbit hanging in the scullery, she reminded herself and since the weather had been cold, it should still be in fresh condition. She decided to try making a rabbit pie and when it was put before them she would observe their reactions, but in case either of them found it not to their liking they could have potatoes and herring or roast crabs. Nothing need be wasted, she told herself. Her husband had enjoyed pastry at *ISLAY*. She herself enjoyed pastry, and if her brother-in-law found it unpalatable, what wasn't eaten could be mixed with the hens' mash.

When the two men got back the pie, with its crisp, gravy-stained crust was keeping hot on the hob alongside a dish of roasted potatoes hot and golden and glistening. Ruari sniffed curiously while he was taking off his boots and oilskins but forbore to comment. He threw a folded oilskin and a pair of gumboots on to the bench.

'There now, do they please you?' he asked.

'Indeed they do,' she responded, putting her feet tentatively into the boots and measuring the oilskin against her. 'I like them fine.' She smiled approvingly. 'They will be gey useful on the moors.' In the city she would have been more gushing but now, in the Islands she knew that even heartfelt appreciation must be expressed laconically.

She put the pie and the roast potatoes on the table. She thought they both looked and smelled delicious.

'My, my!' said her husband. 'What do we have here?' He looked pleased.

'I cleaned out the range this morning and I got lots of stale ash from under the oven. When I lit the fire again the oven got hot enough to cook pastry. I'd seen the rabbit hanging in the scullery and knowing you liked pastry I thought I would make a rabbit pie. The potatoes I roasted because you said you liked them that way,' she reminded him, putting a helping of pie and some roast potatoes on his plate. She turned enquiringly to her brother-in-law but he had ignored the meal on the table and was already helping himself from the pan of potatoes on the hob. Disappointed, she put a portion of the pie on to her own plate and began to eat her meal in silence.

'This is good!' her husband complimented her. 'I like it fine. You should take a taste of it, Ruari Mhor. You would like it,' he urged his brother as he helped himself to another portion.

'Ach, I like to eat fish when I come in from the sea,' was the chilling response.

'I could bake other pies if you would like that,' she said. 'I could make tarts and shortbread and puddings. I could even make bread if you could bring me some yeast.'

'Aye indeed?' he queried.

'I believe we would use a good many more peats to heat the oven regularly but I used to work in the peats for my Granny and I could do so again for you,' she volunteered.

'There is plenty of peat on the wee Island I showed you yesterday,' he said, with rapidly ebbing interest.

He had brought a newspaper back with him from the mainland and was settling himself to read it. She picked up her knitting and, since her brother-in-law had left the kitchen, she settled in the other chair. When the hour of her usual bedtime came round she said, 'Ruari, I am going to make my hot milk. Is there anything you would like me to get for you before I go to bed?'

'No, no,' he declined. 'I will make myself a mug of tea after I have walked my brother's back for him.'

She thought she had misheard him. 'Walk your brother's back, did you say?' she asked banteringly.

114

'Indeed. That is what I said,' he answered gravely.

'But why do you do that?' She was perplexed.

'My brother gets a very sore back sometimes and I walk it for him to give him relief from the pain,' he explained.

'You're telling me he lies down just and you walk on his back?'

He nodded. 'Very lightly and with bare feet,' he elucidated.

She was bewildered. 'And you are saying his back is troubling him tonight?'

'It is so. I could see by his face that he was suffering even before he spoke of it to me.'

'Does this happen very often?' she probed. 'And is there anything I can prepare for you to take to him?'

'Nothing,' he told her. 'And he will be best pleased if you say nothing to him of what I have told you tonight. He will not admit that there can be anything wrong with him.'

'No, I shan't say anything but can't you get him to see a doctor?'

'Never till two Sabbaths meet,' he said. 'My brother will have no doctor near him.' He rose from his chair and swung the kettle over the glowing peats. 'He will be glad of a mug of tea and a dram and by morning I doubt he will be himself again.'

She filled her mug with hot milk and started towards the bedroom.

'I will try not to wake you when I come to bed,' he said. 'You will be tired, will you not?' Could she detect a note of regret in his voice or was he giving himself an excuse for his avoidance of her?

'Fairly tired,' she agreed.

In bed she found herself pondering the character of her brother-in-law. Had there been, at some time in his life, a tragic event or perhaps some tragic circumstances that had caused his features to set so grimly? Or could it be that there was some lurking illness which was betraying his apparent robustness? And could she, instead of striving to be indifferent to his presence, bear with his impassivity and scrutinize his appearance more caringly so as to be able to read the signs of pain on his face? Perhaps then she would be able to understand his attitude towards her.

She was still awake when Ruari came to bed but she feigned sleep and he did not disturb her.

After one of their trips to the mainland, Ruari brought news of a forthcoming wedding.

'A grand wedding too it's to be,' he declared. 'It will be at the church and there's to be a meal following at the hotel.'

'A young couple?' Kirsty enquired. Since it was unlikely she knew either the bride or the bridegroom or any of their relatives, it was the only aspect of the wedding she was interested in.

'Young enough,' Ruari said. 'Willy, that's the bridegroom, is younger than myself and the lassie's not much more than twenty-seven or eight.' He thought for a moment. 'You will wish to be there?' he asked.

She was somewhat taken aback. 'I? No, of course not,' she denied. 'I have not been invited, surely?'

He produced an envelope from his pocket. ' "Mr & Mrs MacDonald and Ruari Mhor MacDonald",' he pointed out, displaying the envelope.

'Will they be relatives of yours?' she asked.

'In a way, I suppose,' he replied dubiously.

'It is very kind of them to include me,' she said.

'How could they not? You will be welcomed. Several folks have said to me that you must be a real hardy to agree to come and live on Westisle and they will want to hear from yourself how you are liking it.'

'Curiosity just,' she commented with a smile. 'Tell me, when is this wedding to be?'

'Thursday week,' he told her. 'At eleven in the morning.'

'And you intend going?'

'If it is not too stormy,' he replied. 'And you must come

too. They might get to thinking you are too swanky to want their company.'

'Then I must certainly come,' she said. 'But Ruari, how will we get a wedding present for them in time for Thursday week?' she demanded.

He looked vague. 'A wedding present?' he repeated.

'Is it not the custom to give a wedding present when one goes to a wedding?' she asked, but even while speaking she was reminding herself that there had been no talk of a wedding in any way connected with the village during the period of her childhood. Was present-giving only a custom of the city?

Ruari's dubious expression cleared. 'Ach, I will put a pound or two in an envelope and give it to Willy on the day,' he said nonchalantly.

'And will I need to give the bride something?'

'A kiss and a handshake only,' he said with a grin.

'Will I not be expected to contribute anything to the meal?' she pressed. 'I shouldn't wish to be thought mean.'

'Nothing. It is the men only who give at weddings,' he assured her solemnly, adding as an afterthought, 'They tell me the bride's aunt who used to work in a hotel in Glasgow is to make a grand bride cake dressed with icing.'

'It sounds interesting,' she said, and began to look forward to the event.

The day before the wedding, when she was attending the cattle it struck her that one of the cows appeared to be a little uneasy and did not come for her allowance of hay. She could see nothing wrong with it but it worried her enough to speak of it when the two brothers came in from the evening's fishing.

'Ach, maybe she's about to calve,' Ruari suggested casually. 'Did you notice if the beast looked near calving? It's early enough yet but the bull's running with them and the winter's been open enough.'

'I wouldn't be able to tell if a cow was near calving,' she told him. 'I was never taught the signs to look for even to tell if a cow was pregnant,' she said flippantly. A few moments went by before she added seriously, 'I think perhaps I'd best stay here and not go to the wedding tomorrow,' she said. 'Maybe the other cows will trouble her.'

A look of irritation crossed Ruari's face. 'How long has she been troubling you?' he asked.

'Oh, just since this morning. I didn't notice anything wrong yesterday.'

'Ach, then there is nothing to be fretting yourself about. She will be able to take care of herself. Will that not be the way of it, Ruari Mhor?' he challenged his brother.

Kirsty shot an anxious glance at her brother-in-law who, though he still persisted in ignoring her, had now yielded sufficiently to sit at the table and share their evening meal. As always, in her presence, he answered his brother's question with merely a nod but instead of the frigidly impassive nod she was accustomed to seeing, she detected in it more than a trace of confirmation.

The morning dawned calm and bright and fearing the wedding celebrations might tempt the brothers to linger on the mainland until after darkness, she decided to pay the cattle an early visit. She would have time, she judged, if they were not too far away, to milk the one cow, feed the rest and ascertain the condition of the beast which had been causing her some concern. When she reached them she saw that the one she had thought to be sick was still distancing itself from the rest of the herd and that it showed no inclination to come for its share of hay but on closer inspection she could see the trail of albumen hanging from its vulva. She is near calving, she told herself, and someone ought to keep an eye on her. She hurried back to the house where the two Ruaris, suitably, if not smartly dressed, were outside polishing their boots.

'No calf?' her husband greeted her.

'No, I didn't see one,' she answered, 'but she's near to it.' She described the albumen. 'I'd far sooner stay and keep an eye on her than go to this wedding. I shall find myself worrying about her.'

'The tide!' she heard her brother-in-law say brusquely. Kirsty looked to her husband for enlightenment.

'Ach, I'm saying there's no need for worry,' he soothed. 'The tide is high now and we have a belief hereabouts that a Highland cow will never drop her calf during an ebb tide. Seeing she hadn't dropped her calf by the time you left she will hold it until the turn of the tide and that will not be before five this evening. We shall have left the wedding behind us by then.'

'Truly?' she questioned.

'As true as I'm here,' he asserted. 'But make haste now and put on your wedding clothes and get yourself quickly down to the boat,' he urged her.

The day was windless, the sea virtually waveless and the crossing to the mainland was so serene she could imagine the boat was gliding through smooth fresh cream. When they reached the modest little church the two Ruaris greeted the few people who had gathered outside but her husband left them to guess who she was. She fixed a steady smile on her face, mumbled a few '*Tha e Breagha*' and followed him into the church where a small organ was being played inexpertly. The bride arrived, the ceremony was performed and in no time at all, it seemed to Kirsty, everyone was walking to the hotel where the reception was being held and where whisky would be available.

It was a good plain meal of chicken and potatoes and turnip followed by jelly and custard; the telegrams, read out by the minister, were satisfyingly lewd and the glasses were recharged unstintingly. When the guests adjourned to the hall – an annexe which, at some future date, was destined to become part of the hotel, a fiddle and melodeon player were waiting to provide the music for dancing. Kirsty was delighted to see Mairi Jane, with whom she had stayed the night before crossing to Westisle, and together they sat on one of the wooden benches that lined the room while they watched the varied antics of the guests. Some danced, some merely stamped their feet in time to the music while others dozed until they fell, amid laughter, from their seats. But whatever they did it was plain that everyone was enjoying the occasion.

When an interval was announced for the musicians to rest and satisfy their thirst, guests were called by name to sing. Some were eager enough, though inevitably a pretence of reluctance was obligatory. Others had to be coaxed, even pulled up from their seats, while between each performance Mairi Jane regaled Kirsty with a brief outline of their genealogies, their circumstances and their rumoured idiosyncrasies. Kirsty was conscious that she herself must be a focus of discussion and responded by exchanging smiles and nods with everyone who smiled and nodded at her. She doubted if she'd remember more than two or three of them but was confident they would remember her.

When several singers had obliged there was a lull until the name of Jamie Eilidh was called, and it seemed to Kirsty that a discernible instant of tension descended on the room when a young boy of about fourteen years of age stood up and began to sing. It was an old Gaelic tune which she vaguely remembered her Granny singing at times when she was bent over the girdle. The refrain of the song was soon being quietly hummed by everyone in the room as hands beat into laps, feet tapped the floor and old heads swayed rhythmically. When the song had ended and the boy had sat down Kirsty remarked to Mairi Jane, 'That boy has a truly lovely voice and that is a lovely old tune.'

'It is an old tune and I have not heard it sung much for a long time,' Mairi Jane told her. 'I've heard it said that some singers find it too, too,' she sought for a word, 'too kind of fickle,' she explained.

'I can well understand that,' Kirsty agreed. 'It has a fair amount of warbling to be mastered. My Granny had the voice for it but I suppose her voice had grown fairly warbly with age.'

'It is a pity that young Jamie cannot speak as well

as he sings,' Mairi Jane confided. Kirsty looked at her curiously. 'Hasn't he a stammer that will almost clamp his throat when he tries to speak,' Mairie Jane went on.

'How tragic!' Kirsty exclaimed. 'Could he not have had treatment to help him?'

'Maybe he has, maybe he hasn't,' Mairi Jane shrugged.

'He's a very handsome boy,' Kirsty observed. Mairi Jane looked slightly shocked. 'I'm not fancying him if that's what you're thinking,' Kirsty laughed. 'But I do think it's a shame he has such a handicap. Has he any brothers or sisters?'

'No, nor will there be any,' Mairi Jane declared. 'See, I'm telling you, when Jamie was born his mother's brain broke, just. There was nothing anybody could do for her so she was sent away to a kind of Home to be looked after by nuns. Mind you, she was young and her parents were queer enough folks that took little to do with folks here. Not that any of us wanted to do with them,' she added haughtily. 'They were Papists and wouldn't have come to these parts only that he was a vet and was wanting experience.'

'Papists?' Kirsty echoed.

'Fierce Papists,' confirmed Mairi Jane. 'Jamie was left to them to look after but seeing he was a bastard fathered by a Seceder they were ashamed of a daughter who had done such a thing. They left here pretty soon afterwards and nobody heard much of them except that the daughter had passed on and the boy had been sent off when he was hardly more than a bairn to some school where there were only nuns to teach him.'

'What about the child's father? Was he also a Papist?' Kirsty asked.

'He was not!' Mairi Jane said vehemently. 'He was as good a Seceder as his father and mother had been before him.'

'I would have thought a staunch Seceder would have avoided any contact with a Papist,' Kirsty reasoned.

'Ach, but Papist women are said to like the boys and

she liked them too much,' Mairi Jane retorted. 'And this one was known to be a wayward lassie. Going out at night in secret. Teasing the young fellows into taking more whisky than they were used to. It wasn't all that long before she had a bairn in her belly.'

'And the man did not marry her?'

'How would a good Seceder come to marry a Papist?' Mairi Jane derided. 'And how would a fierce Papist come to marry a Seceder?'

Her tone made Kirsty feel guilty for having asked the question.

'But it was his baby,' she pointed out.

'Aye, but the fellow was young and foolish and his father had been over-strict with him. No doubt when his father was changed the fellow went a bit wild for a time.' Mairi Jane shook her head sadly. 'The Dear is to be thanked for taking his mother a year or so before her son was named as the father of the lassie's child. She was a fine woman, a good Seceder, a good wife to her husband and a good mother to her family and I believe she would be curdling in her grave still at the very idea of such a thing happening in her family.'

Kirsty, wondering how the time was going, had begun looking around for a clock when she was suddenly aware that her husband had entered the room and was peering around for her. She raised her hand and he responded by beckoning her. She had not seen a sign of either him or her brother-in-law since she had come into the annexe, and had assumed they preferred to be in the fresh air discussing cattle prices and fishing prospects with friends and colleagues, rather than taking part in the festivities in the closeness of the crowded annexe.

She took her leave of Mairi Jane, gave her warmest good wishes to the bride – the bridegroom had disappeared – included the guests in a cheery farewell wave and followed her husband down to the boat. The sea was ruffled now by only a whisper of evening breeze and when they reached the house the peat fire was still smouldering promisingly.

She said, 'I will go to look at the cattle before I cook a meal, if that is all right with you.'

Ruari mumbled approval. Her brother-in-law said, 'You will not be needing to cook a meal after all we've eaten this day, surely? A bowl of porridge will suit you surely, Ruari Beag?'

Kirsty gaped at him. He had actually spoken to her. Ruari Beag flashed her a cautious glance as if warning her not to show too much surprise.

'I will go and change my clothes ready to go to the cows,' she said tonelessly.

The kitchen was empty when she returned and she headed straight for the moors. The cow she'd been anxious about was not with the herd but hearing a shout she looked towards a small hillock where her husband was standing and waving his arms to attract her attention. She made towards him as fast as she could.

'See!' he announced and as she approached him she saw the cow with her coffee-brown calf nuzzling at her belly, searching for her teats.

'A fine heifer calf,' Ruari said delightedly.

'Oh, you clever girl,' cried Kirsty equally delighted, as she went to fondle the tight-curled coat of the calf. 'What is to be done with them now?' she asked.

'Ach, she'll be fine where she is,' he said. 'We'll wait a minute or two just and make sure it's sucking all right and then we can leave her here. The night is calm and she's got good shelter here if she feels she wants it.' The calf found a teat and started to suck strongly. The mother watched it with tender possessiveness. 'Come away now,' Ruari bade her and together they began to walk back towards the house.

After a little while Kirsty asked, 'Ruari, your brother spoke to me in quite a friendly way tonight. What has happened to make him do that? Do you think he's getting over his dislike of me?'

124

'Didn't I tell you he would come round before very long?' he stated. 'He has never disliked you, he just misunderstood you and thought you wouldn't settle for the sort of life we have here. You proved him wrong when you said you would stay here rather than go to the wedding. He admitted it when we were coming out this evening to look at the cow.'

'He was there, too? I didn't see him.'

'No, he left when he saw you coming. He took the other way back to the house.'

'I don't care about his avoiding me but it will make for a much pleasanter atmosphere in the house if the three of us can speak together.'

'Aye indeed,' Ruari agreed. 'But you must mind he is not a man for much talk at any time,' he warned.

'I shan't expect much talk,' she rejoined. 'Just a recognition of my presence.' She began to feel light-hearted and started to sing quietly to herself thinking, because he was a few paces in front, he would not hear her. He paused until she caught up with him.

'You were glad to be at the wedding?'

'Yes, I enjoyed it much more than I'd expected to. What about you? I hardly saw you or your brother all afternoon but I suppose you heard some of what was going on even if you didn't see it.'

'Ach, weren't we making sure the bridegroom was fit for what he had to do,' he told her. 'It's kind of expected when there's a wedding.'

'You mean filled him with whisky?' she jested. He only winked at her.

'You missed some good singing,' she pointed out.

'But there were windows open and we heard quite a bit of it,' he claimed.

'There was a young boy there who had a lovely singing voice but Mairi Jane was telling me he had difficulty in speaking. It seems a great shame. Did you hear him?'

'No, I don't believe we did,' said Ruari noncommittally. 'Maybe we were singing ourselves enough to drown him.'

When they got back to the house her brother-in-law was nowhere to be seen but he appeared in time to take some porridge she'd made. He was still his taciturn self; his gaze still excluded her but the atmosphere was noticeably less strained. Ruari Beag said, 'The tide will not be right for an early start. That is so is it not, Ruari Mhor?'

'That is so,' his brother confirmed.

'I will be as well off in my bed then,' said Ruari Beag as he rose from the table and went through to the bedroom.

Kirsty took the used bowls into the scullery, washed them, measured some milk into a saucepan and returned to the kitchen. She'd expected her brother-in-law would have taken himself off to his own room as was his usual habit and was surprised to find him still sitting contemplatively beside the range. Ignoring him she heated her milk, poured it into a mug and sat herself down in the opposite chair. He appeared not to notice her and since it was the first time she had been alone with him she felt a little uneasy. As she sipped at her milk the desire to speak to him grew more insistent. At length she blurted out, 'Ruari Mhor, please listen to what I have to tell you.' He did not look at her nor did his expression change. 'Please bear with me when I plead with you not to let me come between you and your brother. I have pleaded with him and he tells me everything will be all right, but let me tell you I would not have agreed to marry him had I suspected you would be so vexed by it, and I promise I will take my leave if you cannot find it in your heart to accept my presence here.'

He still did not speak. Her own voice strengthened. 'I understand you believe Ruari Beag to have acted very foolishly in marrying me and bringing me here, but I must tell you that your brother has been very kind to me and I have sworn to do my best to make him happy, but now I well know that this will be impossible if I am allowed to come between him and you.' She drew a deep quivering breath, finished her milk and stood up. She felt so much better for having confronted him on the subject even if, as she suspected, he had not listened to a word she had spoken.

He stood up and went towards the door of the kitchen but there he stopped and turned round to face her. 'Kirsty MacLennan,' he told her sternly. 'I believe my brother to have been foolish in marrying you and bringing you to this Island.' He paused a second and then added, 'It is not the first foolish thing he has done.'

'But I am learning to love Westisle,' she objected. There were tears in her eyes and she blinked them quickly away.

'I say again it is no place for a woman,' he stated, and went into the passage, closing the door behind him.

She piled dry peats on the dying fire and topped them with a few wet ones before she went to bed, and she was surprised when she entered the room to see that Ruari was still awake.

'I thought you were tired,' she commented, as she uncoiled her hair and twisted it into the usual two plaits. As she was getting into bed beside him he pulled at one of the plaits playfully.

'You enjoyed the wedding, you were saying?' her husband asked her again.

'I did,' she admitted, pulling the bedclothes around her. She tensed herself when he reached to pull them away.

'I believe Willy and his bride will be enjoying themselves now,' he muttered, his whisky-wet mouth on her ear. His face was bristly on her cheeks, his hot rough hands were urgently exploring her thighs. She told herself to yield. He was not gentle. She winced with the hurt of it but the interlude was mercifully brief and when he'd turned away from her she lay still, listening to his steady breathing while she questioned her own mixed reactions to the experience. She hadn't enjoyed it, she concluded, but she was glad she'd had the experience. If there had been love between them, she thought, it might have been a more joyous experience for her, but if it satisfied him she was content that it should be so. What a day it had

127

been, she reflected. A real red-letter-day. First a new calf had been born, next she had been to a wedding, then her brother-in-law had broken his silence and now she was no longer a virgin. There was a smug smile on her face as she drifted off to sleep.

She rose early next morning and went to the cattle before Ruari was awake. She was searching for a missing hen when he appeared dressed ready to go to sea.

'I'm away,' he called, and gestured a farewell. She watched him go and wondered if he felt any lingering excitement after what had happened last night. He did not even glance her way. She continued her search for the hen, which she found eventually sitting on a full brood of eggs in a cosy nest inside an old barrel. Two days later she found another hen also sitting tight on a clutch of eggs. If they all hatched she realised they would soon have an over-abundance of hens.

She mentioned the likelihood to Ruari when they were having supper one night.

'We'll not be wanting any more eggs. Haven't we plenty already?' he retorted.

'Couldn't we sell eggs on the mainland?' she proposed.

'It's best to wring the necks of any we don't need.'

'Oh, surely not,' she protested. 'We can eat the cockerels but to wring the necks of the pullets seems a terrible waste to me.'

'More eggs means more feeding,' he pointed out.

'But if I sell eggs on the mainland the money would pay for extra feed. It isn't as if we'd have to buy much extra because the flock here is almost self-supporting,' she argued.

She left it three or four weeks before she mentioned the subject again, and by that time there were nineteen more chickens cheeping around their mothers.

'Have you thought any more about taking eggs to the mainland?' she asked.

This time it was her brother-in-law who answered her question. 'We will take eggs to the mainland but we will not do the selling,' he stated. 'You must come with us to do that and what money you make by doing so you can keep for yourself. Hens is women's work. We will not be concerned with such things.'

Kirsty was overcome with surprise. 'I'm not wanting to take money for myself but maybe I can spend a little on cheering up this room? Maybe some new covering for the floor and also some curtains for the window?' Her husband looked at her wide-eyed, obviously seeing nothing that needed improvement. Her brother-in-law merely grunted.

'Will I do that?' she pressed.

Ruari Beag looked at his brother before saying, 'If that is what you wish.'

Kirsty grew quite excited about the prospect of going on regular trips to the mainland and selling eggs. It meant she wouldn't be completely shut off from shops as she was on Westisle, and though the shops were small and scattered it would be a welcome break for her to meet and perhaps familiarize herself with the people. She'd been lavish recently in her use of eggs, simply so as not to see them wasted, but now she decided to be more frugal.

The weeks and months went by. She encouraged more hens to 'clock' as the warmer weather came, and gradually built up the flock until she was able to take a full basket of eggs each time she made the trip to the mainland. She pored over the mail order catalogues and sent off for material to make curtains and cushions. She bought new linoleum for the floor and bright new waxcloth for the table. Slowly the kitchen began to look a little like the room she had envisaged when she'd first seen it. She'd got the two brothers to move the dresser from the scullery into the kitchen and, after staining and varnishing it she'd filled its shelves with the plain, everyday pottery she'd found in the scullery. Then one day, when she'd mentioned she needed wool for mending his sweater, Ruari suddenly thought to look in one of the chests which had been in the bedroom but had since been stored in a room where Ruari Mhor kept his books and gramophone.

Kirsty gasped with pleasure. There was certainly mending wool in the chest, but much of it was interposed between brightly coloured cups and saucers, tea plates and fruit bowls.

'The Laird's wife left them to my mother. It was she who packed them away.'

'But these would look lovely on the dresser,' she pleaded.

'Take them and do whatever you like with them,' Ruari said, and when he came back that evening and saw them on the dresser shelves he congratulated her with an approving, 'Aye, aye.'

She was thrilled. The kitchen had been transformed and the brothers had accepted it with never a single word of criticism.

Her life on Westisle settled into a fairly regular pattern. She cooked, cleaned, washed, mended, knitted and sewed. No matter the weather conditions she trekked daily over the moors to attend the cows, and though she would not have claimed the trek was invariably a rewarding experience, she came to look upon the task more as a mission she was glad to accomplish. She looked after the hens. In the spring she lent a hand at the kelp gathering; she helped with the seasonal planting and harvesting. She dug a piece of land for a vegetable garden and worked it herself. Whenever she looked it seemed there was always work asking to be done but her life was so satisfying she rarely felt tired. The two brothers neither cosseted her nor did they make any attempt to burden her with more work. Instead they quietly accepted only what she volunteered to do. Kirsty counted herself more than lucky.

One day when she was over on the mainland to sell eggs she met Mairi Jane and in the uninviting looking 'tea-room' they had a cup of tea and a bannock.

'There's talk of asking Padruig to bring some of the folk on an evening cruise,' Mairi Jane told her. 'You'll not say no to that?'

'A cruise to Westisle?' Kirsty echoed. 'I certainly

wouldn't want to say no.' She caught her breath for a moment. 'I suppose even the two Ruaris would welcome it.'

'Ach them!' Mairi Jane derided. 'They'd no doubt be glad of some company to take a look at their beautiful Island. They think there's no place like it.'

'I'm beginning to feel the same way about it myself,' Kirsty confided. Mairi Jane flashed her an enigmatic smile.

'When is the cruise likely to be?' Kirsty asked.

'I would say the first calm evening when Padruig has nothing better to do,' was the reply.

'I just want to make sure I have plenty of scones baked,' Kirsty said. 'But tell me, Mairi Jane, is it likely to be a boatload or just a half dozen?'

'I would say more likely a boatload,' Mairi Jane informed her. 'But you will have plenty of time to put the girdle on the fire when you see the boat coming, or even when you hear the laughing and singing. There's plenty of that goes on when there's one of these evening cruises.'

'Will you be coming?' Kirsty asked eagerly.

'I will certainly come and see what you have made of your home,' Mairi Jane promised.

'I shall be looking forward to it,' Kirsty said warmly.

The two brothers had already heard about the proposed evening cruise and as soon as they got back from fishing the next day they started to hide anything that was likely to be 'borrowed' by members of the cruise party. Kirsty looked enquiringly at her husband. 'Ach, they see a thing they'd like to try out and then they ask if they can have a lend of it. When you come to use it yourself it's not there but when you ask them where it is they think they've returned it. It makes Ruari Mhor fairly cross at times so it's best not to leave things where folks can see them. That way they don't ask for a lend of them.'

As Mairi Jane had predicted, they were able to hear the cruise boat approaching before they could see it.

'They're on their way,' shouted her husband, coming

towards the house. 'And there's a good load of them.' His voice was unusually excited.

The evening was calm and sun-goldened; gulls were winging lazily towards their chosen night haunts; from somewhere on the Island came the sound of snipe drumming and as Kirsty set out to welcome her visitors she could hear a chorus of happy voices mingling with the late calls of the gulls. The boat was well down in the water with its load of bodies. I hope it doesn't blow up before they go home, she thought as she greeted them and helped some of the older ones over the rough shingle. There were loud splashings as several of the younger ones, in a hurry to be first ashore, missed their footing but their plights produced even more shouting and laughter.

Kirsty led the way to the house where there were kettles simmering on the range, teapots warming on the fender and piles of buttered girdle scones, oatcakes, bannock and shortbread covering the table. The women sat on whatever chairs or benches were available, the men on the floor and the younger people either did likewise or brought three or four dry peats from the stack and used them as stools. Inevitably the teasing and chaffing, the gossip and the story-telling prompted the desire to break into song and soon the kitchen was filled with singing, chanting and humming voices; not loud but mellowed as if in deference to the serenity of the evening. And then came a voice she could recognise. She'd been so busy seeing that people were well looked after that she'd not paid much attention to the youngsters in the party, but when the boy she knew as Jamie Eilidh began to sing she was captivated. When he'd sung one song it was she who called for more. She spoke directly to him. 'You have a splendid voice, Jamie Eilidh, and I could listen to you for many an hour without getting tired of it.'

He blushed but he did not answer.

Her brother-in-law stirred himself from where he had been standing by the open door. 'The tide is right and the breeze is rising. I'm thinking you'd best be on your way if you're not going to stay here till morning.'

'My, my,' they chorused and began making their way towards the door. As they departed they were full of praise for Kirsty's baking and when she invited them to fill their pockets they left the table quite bare.

She accompanied them to where the men of the party were gathered around the boat.

'We'll be back,' they promised as the boat left. 'Oh, you must do that,' she cried fervently. 'I've enjoyed myself so much.'

Someone on the boat began to sing 'Will ye no come back again?' and Kirsty, who had never considered that she had a pleasing voice, joined in, holding out her arms in an ecstatic way in response to their waved farewells. 'They'd best not do much of that or they'll sink the boat,' said Ruari Beag. 'You'd best not encourage them by staying here.'

Reluctantly she followed him along the path until they reached the higher ground where she paused to feast her eyes on the breathtaking beauty of the scene. The sea was turquoise; the sunset seemed to be in possession of the whole wide horizon while over the gaunt dark hills of the mainland a slim crescent of moon peeped like a young breast emerging from a torn gown. Whoever would want to live in a city, she asked herself.

On fine Saturday mornings it was now the custom for the two Ruaris to take their catch early to the mainland, putting Kirsty ashore to dispose of her basket of eggs while they stayed around the fish pier to watch their lobsters being auctioned, to supervise the boat being tanked up with fuel ready for the following week's fishing, and to make a leisurely inspection of other boats and their catches, after which they adjourned with the other fishermen to discuss prices over a dram at the hotel.

Quite often on these Saturday visits Kirsty might meet Mairi Jane, and if there had been no warning to hurry back to the pier they would go for a session to the local tea-room. On the Saturday following the cruise party she was hailed by Mairi Jane and a group of her friends and it was only a minute or two before they were heading for the tea-room. It was then that she heard about Jamie Eilidh's plans for the future.

'Wasn't he with your brother-in-law outside your house while the ceilidh was taking place, and then only this morning my man was saying the boy was going to learn about fishing from the two Ruaris.'

They could see from her surprised expression that she knew nothing of the proposal. 'Are you saying that Jamie Eilidh is going to be a fisherman in *The Two Ruaris?*' Kirsty exclaimed. 'Does he want to be a fisherman?'

'What else would he be fit for after being taught by nuns?' one of the women asked aggressively.

'Really,' Kirsty countered, 'I've heard nuns make very good teachers. I've met lots of scholars who could boast of being taught by nuns.'

'Not young fellows with stammers,' the woman derided.

'Oh, be quiet!' Mairi Jane reprehended the woman

134

mildly. 'No, the trouble is that the boy's stammer is not likely to help him find work in these parts except at the fishing, and it's in these parts he wishes to stay. Folks tell me he has a good brain and is good with his hands. They say he can sort things like broken cameras and broken wireless sets given the chance – but what use are skills like that in this kind of place?'

'I could do with someone to sort my wireless set,' Kirsty muttered.

'Likely he'll do that,' Mairi Jane proposed.

'Has he left school?' Kirsty asked.

'Didn't he leave school last week just, at the beginning of the holidays? That's why he's round about the pier a lot.'

'Is his home here, then?' Kirsty probed.

'Not here just,' one of the women replied. 'He has an uncle at Rubhana that he stays with when he's not at school. But there's talk that the uncle's thinking of marrying again and taking himself off somewhere. His new wife doesn't want to have Jamie with them.'

Mairi Jane permitted herself a short sigh. 'Though he's been brought up a Papist I can find it in my heart to feel sorry for the boy. Since the day he was created he's never been wanted.'

They finished their tea, collected their various bags and went their separate ways. Kirsty met the two Ruaris on the pier. She was surprised neither of them had mentioned to her that Jamie was to join them on the boat, but since she'd never had anything to do with the boat she assumed they'd taken it for granted she was not interested.

When they were back on Westisle in the late afternoon the boat was moored and since neither of the brothers would set foot on her again until the Sabbath was safely over, they tackled odd jobs which had accumulated during their time at sea. Ruari Beag was over by the barn mending creels. Ruari Mhor was working on the fence for her vegetable garden. Seeing it was a bright calm day Kirsty began to clean the windows. She called to her brother-in-

135

law, 'Ruari Mhor, I was shamed just by the state of these windows when the folks were here last night. It was that wind earlier in the week that drove the rain and spray up from the sea and I was too stupid to notice it until the sun had dried it. It is not easy scrubbing it off with just wet cloths and I have not yet found this special kind of moss you yourself use.' When there was no response she ventured to ask, 'Will you not bring some for me next time you are near it?'

When he turned to look at her she thought his face looked grey and drawn and suspected his back was troubling him.

'I will not get moss for you,' he said curtly. 'But you will tell me when you wish the windows to be cleaned and I will do it.'

'I know I'm not a good hand at cleaning windows but I'm not trying to get out of doing it,' she argued.

'I have always cleaned the windows,' he snapped.

Kirsty shrugged her shoulders and went inside to start baking for the Sabbath.

She herself was no longer the strict Sabbatarian she had been brought up to be and though she still shunned the idea of sewing or knitting or doing other such handicrafts on the Sabbath it was more superstition than religion that disallowed it. But she had, during the years in the city, become used to cooking a good midday meal on Sundays. On Westisle it seemed practical to continue doing so and since there was no hint of a grumble from her husband or her brother-in-law she'd simply carried on. She got the impression they liked the experience of enjoying a lazy afternoon and using a full stomach as an excuse for their inertia. But for Kirsty, Saturday baking evenings had also become a kind of ritual and this again seemed to fit easily into her weekly timetable. There was no doubt the two Ruaris enjoyed her baking. Her husband sometimes asked her to make 'another of those sweetie tarts' or 'some of those jammy rolls' or other delights she had produced from the now well-behaved oven. Both men proved they

136

were incredibly 'sweet-toothed' and it gave her pleasure to see them reaching for goodie after goodie until the plates and tins were almost empty.

It was not until they were finishing their Sunday dinner next day that she mentioned casually, 'I heard yesterday that the boy Jamie Eilidh is to come aboard *The Two Ruaris* to learn about fishing.'

The two men locked glances for a second before Ruari Mhor answered, 'That is so.'

'Will he be useful to you, or are you just offering him the chance of work?' she asked.

'He will be useful,' Ruari Beag said positively.

'If he is not seasick he will be useful,' confirmed Ruari Mhor. 'And if he is not clumsy enough to fall overboard.'

'Can he swim, d'you know?' she queried.

'He says he's got certificates for swimming.'

'He might prove to be an asset on the boat,' Kirsty said. 'Will he be starting tomorrow?'

'Maybe, maybe,' Ruari Beag allowed.

It was plain they were not intending to discuss the matter further, and though she would have liked to ask if they would be bringing Jamie to the house for his evening meal, she forbore from putting the question. She stood up and started to clear the table. The brothers wandered outside and hearing their fading voices she guessed they had gone to find their favourite sites to lie down and look at the sky while they digested their dinner. Kirsty washed the dishes, changed into her black dress and then taking a book, a rug and a pillow, sought her own favourite spot behind the barn.

The following Saturday morning when she took her basket of eggs down to the boat she found Jamie already aboard. 'How?' she asked her husband.

'Jamie sleeps aboard,' he said. 'There are good bunks that are not used,' he added, 'and it is handy to know there is somebody on board when she is left, in case of trouble.'

'What sort of trouble?'

'Oh, she might drag her anchor or she might . . .'

'But what could Jamie by himself do about such things?' she interrupted.

'Ach, he could throw out another anchor to keep her, while he swims ashore to get us.'

'He can swim, then? You know that for sure?'

'He's a great one for the swimming,' he assured her. 'He talks of trying to swim across the Sound before he's much older.'

'Maybe he's aiming to be a champion swimmer and become famous,' she suggested lightly. She would have liked to talk to Jamie but thought it would perhaps be cruel when he was too confused even to acknowledge her smile.

She said when they had returned to the house, 'I think it would be a good idea to bring Jamie here for a bite to eat in the evenings. He would not be able to cook aboard the boat, would he?'

'There is a Primus aboard,' Ruari Beag said. 'And there is plenty of bread and butter and tea. He does well enough.'

'Maybe it's fine in the good weather but when the autumn comes it will not be much of a home for him. Can we not turn the small room where the packing cases are stored into a bedroom so he can live with us here? I shan't complain at having a little extra cooking to do.'

'Aye, we can do that but will he come?' her husband posed the question.

'We can try him,' she said. 'But let's get him used to taking his meal with us here as a first step.'

It appeared that Jamie was by no means averse to coming to the house for a meal, and it was not long before he was helping to clear out the small room. Kirsty showed him her wireless. 'They tell me you are good at sorting wireless sets, is that so?' He nodded eagerly. 'How about having a go at sorting this one?' Again he nodded so she left it with him, reflecting that since it was no good to her as it was it would be no loss if he made a mess of it.

So Jamie was installed in what had been a lumber room and Kirsty revelled in having four people at the table for meals. It was almost like a family, she thought. And she particularly liked having a youngster to feed: a youngster who had a good appetite and who appreciated her cooking: a youngster who enjoyed 'sorting' things. He'd sorted her wireless set though reception on Westisle proved to be barely audible and totally erratic. Since his hearing seemed to be more acute than hers she told him to keep the set and on winter evenings he would bend over it, the headphones over his ears and exclaiming whenever he managed to pick up a word or two of what was being broadcast. His stammer was improving and she remarked on the improvement to her husband.

'Aye, well, he'll be bound to lose it at sea. When you're feared of something it's no good shouting for help if you've got a stammer,' he mocked.

'Is he turning out to be any good at the fishing?' she asked the two Ruaris one evening.

'No bad, no bad at all,' murmured Ruari Beag.

'He does well enough,' granted her brother-in-law. 'He can bait creels, I'll say that for him.'

'I'm asking because he likes fine to come to the cattle with me when he's not at sea. And he's learned how to milk,' Kirsty told them. 'I'm thinking the day might come when he will forsake the sea for the land.'

'Maybe, maybe,' Ruari Beag agreed indifferently.

The winter was coarse but the house was cosy enough since there was now always a good fire to ensure the oven was hot. It was too wild for fishing and for week after week the boat lay hauled up in the shelter of Glen Roag. But as soon as spring brought gentler seas and longer hours of daylight the two Ruaris, with visibly rising spirits loaded the creels which Jamie had baited aboard the boat and headed out to sea.

Kirsty felt an upsurge of her own spirits and she busied herself with the spring cleaning, the annual blanket washing and the planting of her garden which had yielded well enough the previous year. The hens had got over their winter sulk had begun to lay again, calves were born, and when the men returned from fishing they dug the ground for potatoes, sowed corn and if there was still daylight, crossed to the adjacent Island to cut peats for the following winter.

Kirsty had realised that she was using far more peats than the two brothers must have thought necessary, since before she came they'd needed to keep only a frugal fire of smouldering embers while they were out fishing. She'd volunteered to help by throwing out the peats as they were cut but they'd refused her help saying they worked better on their own. Now Jamie was available they appeared to be keen enough to have his help. It was just herself they preferred to do without, she realised and though she hadn't resented their refusal it had deepened her feeling of being a woman of no consequence. They had made it plain that they had managed without help before her arrival and they would manage again if she was not there. Perhaps life might be a little less comfortable for them but they had been so accustomed to discomfort they would easily get used to it again. She'd been useful to them, but being useful didn't mean being wanted, and more than anything she would like to have felt wanted. The thought set her to wondering if Jamie felt the same way.

The next time she met Mairi Jane, Kirsty said, 'As soon as the spring work is finished I shall be expecting you to be over on an evening cruise.'

'And aren't folks speaking of it already?' replied Mairi Jane. 'They fairly enjoyed the last one and they're saying the weather is set fair for a week or so. I've no doubt you'll be seeing them soon enough.'

'It can't be too soon,' Kirsty invited.

It was early the following week when they arrived and this time they had with them not only the bride and bridegroom but also the man who'd played the melodeon at the wedding. As soon as they were gathered in the house and had satisfied themselves with tea and scones the melodeon was produced and it was not long before the younger folks were dancing barefoot on the grass outside the house. Jamie, very much less shy than he had been the previous year, had joined the dancers and seeing him Mairi Jane observed that Kirsty had 'likely undone the harm the nuns had done him'. Kirsty accepted the observation with an ironic smile.

She went into the house to brew more tea for the thirsty dancers. Mairi Jane followed her. '*Mo ghaoil*,' she said, 'will you not sit down while I brew the tea? You are not looking yourself tonight.'

'I think there must be thunder hanging around,' Kirsty answered her. 'I felt a little dizzy and headachey this morning.'

'And thunder affects you?' Mairi Jane looked at her quizzically.

'I'm afraid it does,' Kirsty admitted. 'It did when I was living in the city anyway.' She filled one of the teapots and Mairi Jane filled another before going to the door calling 'Strupak!' The dancers came crowding back into the kitchen.

It was after midnight when they left, but the peaks of the hills were still gilded by the afterglow of sunset. Mairi Jane, as she kissed Kirsty '*Oidhche Mhath!*' asked if she would be over with her eggs the following Saturday. 'Why, yes,' Kirsty assured her. 'The hens are laying well again now.'

'Ask will the two Ruaris give you leave to stay overnight in my house,' she surprised Kirsty by saying. 'We are having a wee ceilidh and concert in the village hall and you would do well to come. There is to be a singer who's won prizes at the Mod and a wee dancing girl who's won prizes at the games. It will be good entertainment.'

'I'd love to come but it will mean one of them having to milk the cow on Sunday.'

'And cannot Jamie milk the cow?' she asked.

Kirsty blinked at her momentary forgetfulness. 'Why,

yes, I'm sure Jamie would like to milk the cow. I've taught him how to do it and he's keen enough when he's not at sea. The trouble is, I doubt if either of the two Ruaris will agree to use the boat on the Sabbath to come to get me.'

'Not on the Sabbath but on the Monday morning when they've finished at the lobsters surely?'

'I'll put it to them,' Kirsty promised.

The two Ruaris made no demur at all when she did put it to them and young Jamie jumped at the idea of milking the cow, so on Saturday Kirsty packed her nightdress and a new blouse and skirt she had made for herself, safely under the eggs in her basket and, warning the two Ruaris and Jamie not to forget to call for her on the Monday morning, she set off to get the bus to Mairi Jane's house.

She enjoyed the concert but found the hall stuffy and had to go outside during the interval to cool herself down. She found herself wishing for a moment or two that she was going back to Westisle that night so that she would have a cool sea wind to refresh her before she went to her bed. When the concert was over, a friend whom Mairi Jane introduced as Flora MacNee insisted they accompany her back to her cottage for a 'wee strupak'. Kirsty would have liked to forgo the invitation but she knew she must not. There was a porch overlooking the sea at Flora MacNee's house, and there as they sat drinking tea topped with a small measure of whisky they talked of the old days – the old folk and the old ways. It was fascinating but Kirsty's head was heavy with sleep. She saw Mairi Jane regarding her attentively and realised she had not drunk her tea.

'Kirsty has been having a touch of the weather so she says,' Mairi Jane explained to Flora. 'But I'm thinking it's not only the weather that is troubling her just.'

Kirsty glanced at her with eyebrows raised. 'A touch of the sun?' she queried. Mairi Jane said nothing. 'Surely you're not thinking I've caught something or other,' Kirsty joked.

Mairi Jane smiled. 'Flora here is the nurse for the village,' she said. 'What would you say she has caught, Flora?'

'No more than a touch of pregnancy,' said the nurse.

Kirsty was aghast. 'But I'm too old!' Her voice was almost a shriek. 'I'm forty. I can't be pregnant. I started the change three months back.'

'I doubt it's not the change,' the nurse insisted.

Kirsty held her face in her hands. 'How can you be so sure?'

'I cannot be certain but I have nursed a great many pregnant women. The signs strike me the minute I see them. You will soon know if I am right.'

'I can't believe it,' Kirsty protested. 'Not when I'm forty years old.'

'My mother was forty-four when she became pregnant with me,' Mairi Jane interposed.

'My sister was forty-six when she gave birth to her first child,' the nurse added.

Kirsty was voiceless for several minutes and then she pleaded, 'You will not say a word of this to anyone, will you? Least of all to Ruari my husband. I shall wait for a while before I make it known to him.'

The nurse raised her chin proudly. 'You should not have to ask a nurse to keep a secret,' she admonished Kirsty. 'It is part of our training.'

'And you need have no fear that I shall break your secret,' asserted Mairi Jane.

As they walked to Mairi Jane's cottage Kirsty could only converse in stilted monosyllables and when they reached it Mairi Jane, blessedly understanding, made no fuss when she chose to go straight to bed. Kirsty lay with her secret and stroked her palms over her rounded belly. She could detect no swelling; no difference in its normal roundedness. She still could not believe she was pregnant and yet she wanted to believe it. Her age still worried her. Would she be likely to go the full term? As sleep overpowered her she resolved not to speak to her husband about the possibility until her pregnancy had run for at least another couple of months and the signs had become inescapable.

The summer was hot and sunny and the harvest had finished much earlier than usual, so the two Ruaris and Jamie decided to go more frequently to the peat Island to bring back a good stock of peats. She and Jamie collected driftwood from the shore and well before autumn winds threatened to stir the sea to violence they felt satisfied they had plenty of winter fuel within easy reach of the house.

'We shall be nice and snug this winter by the look of it,' she remarked as she saw the two Ruaris putting the finishing touches to the stack. She thought, if there is really going to be a bairn we shall need to be nice and cosy.

Her husband said, 'One can never have too many peats.'

The following Saturday when they were returning from the mainland, although the sea was hardly touched by wind, Kirsty suddenly retched. She tried to be discreet about it and neither her husband nor her brother-in-law appeared to notice anything wrong, but Jamie was concerned. 'Just something I ate at the tea-room,' she excused herself. 'Say nothing about it.'

'Next Sat . . . I c-could t-take this,' he managed to say, gesturing towards the empty egg basket.

She didn't want him to see how profoundly relieved she was. 'I would be glad if you would sometimes do that for me Jamie,' she told him. 'I would have more time to spend doing all the things I need to do before the Sabbath.' He smiled at her warmly.

For six consecutive Saturdays she did not go to the mainland and the brothers, seeing that Jamie was now taking her eggs, asked no questions. But on the seventh Saturday she knew there were some things she must do. Her pregnancy was advancing and she had made few preparations for the birth. She'd pored over catalogues which advertised baby clothes, but imagining the look she would get from the postmistress when she saw the address, she hadn't dared risk posting an order at the fish pier post office. Instead she'd written to Mairi Jane saying she would likely be on the mainland and hoped they would be able to meet. Mairi Jane would then take the money for a postal order and would send it together with a list of baby clothes to the catalogue address from her own post office, and when the order was delivered Mairi Jane would write to her for instructions as to how Kirsty would get it.

They chatted together in the tea-room.

'And your man is pleased?' Mairi Jane asked, and when Kirsty admitted she hadn't yet told Ruari Beag she shook her head disapprovingly.

'I've made up my mind to tell him this very evening,' Kirsty assured her. 'I have promised myself I will do that.'

They were back on the Island earlier than usual, Ruari Beag having mentioned that since the sea was calm they might just as well bring back some more peats from the peat Island. 'No sense in leaving them there to go rotten,' he said.

Ruari Mhor wanted to spend his time working on the engine of the fishing boat, so Jamie went with Ruari Beag and Kirsty started on her baking. She felt a little tense at the thought of telling her husband he might soon be a father. How would he take the news, she wondered. Would he be pleased, or would he be disgusted at the idea? And her brother-in-law? Would he revert to his sulky resentment if he had to put up with a child in the house?

She was lifting a pan from the fire when she heard the sound of boots outside the door and was expecting Ruari Beag and Jamie to appear. Instead it was her brother-in-law. He stood in the doorway staring at her as if he was transfixed. His face looked more agonized than she had yet seen it. Is it his back or has he had an accident, she asked herself. She put down the pan and went hesitantly towards him. 'Ruari Mhor,' she pleaded, 'will you not sit down or lie on your bed? I can see you are in great pain and I will go and find Ruari Beag to help you.'

He was still staring at her, and impulsively she extended an arm towards him, thinking he needed help. 'Please,' she began, and pushed a chair close to him, fearing he was about to collapse.

At last he spoke. 'You will not find Ruari Beag,' he said stoically.

'I cannot leave you while I go to find him,' she said. 'Not while you are in such pain.'

'Be quiet, woman. You will not find him,' he repeated.

'But he'll surely be back from the peat Island by now,' she insisted. 'Why wouldn't I find him?'

'The sea has claimed him,' he said flatly.

Her head shot up in alarm.

'The sea?' She thought he was confused. 'What are you saying, Ruari Mhor?' Her hand went to her throat as she stared at the hard set of his jaw. 'Oh, dear God!' she whispered, as what he was telling her pierced her consciousness. She could not stop herself swaying: the kitchen furniture seemed to move as if it was being shaken by an earthquake. When she came to she was lying on her bed and thinking she was just awakening from a bad dream. She sat up and saw her brother-in-law holding a mug of tea towards her but, wordlessly, she shook her head. 'Is it true what you are telling me?' she said faintly.

'It is true,' he said.

'But they only went across to the peat Island and it is a calm evening,' she tried to argue. 'What happened?'

'Jamie tells me he and my brother had a good load of peats on the small boat and were on their way back when Ruari saw a good piece of driftwood a distance away. My brother thought it would be good to carve and wanted to tow it behind the boat, so Jamie jumped in the water and started to swim for it. He didn't see Ruari was having trouble with the outboard motor, but thinking he heard a shout he looked round and was in time to see the wee boat turn over, and though he swam back as fast as he could hoping Ruari would be holding on to the boat there was no Ruari, no boat and no engine. He shouted and dived and swam around searching for long enough before he gave up and swam ashore here on the Island to tell me. I went with him in the fishing boat and we searched again but we knew my brother was gone. We went over to the mainland to let them know and more boats have gone to search. They are still searching.'

'Then I must away and join them. I'm a good swimmer,' she shrilled, getting up from the bed.

'There will be good swimmers there. If he is to be found they will find him. Otherwise we must wait until the sea chooses to give up its dead.'

Distraught, she hurried into the kitchen and began to shift pots and pans about on the range not really knowing why she was doing so.

'Where is Jamie now?' she thought to ask.

'Jamie is down on the shore,' he told her. She looked at him questioningly. 'He is suffering because he was unable to save his father.' He paused for a moment before adding, 'He thinks you might blame him.'

'His father?'

'Jamie is Ruari Beag's son,' he said.

Her voice dried in her throat as she stared up at him. 'His son?' she repeated incredulously.

'He never told you?' Slowly she shook her head in denial. 'He did a foolish thing,' he said. 'It was a long time ago. Try not to blame him.'

She remembered suddenly that Ruari Beag had drowned without knowing about the bairn she was carrying in her belly and the knowledge drove like a blade into her heart. 'I had something to tell him,' she confessed. 'I was going to tell him tonight I am near five months pregnant with his bairn and now he has died without knowing it.' Her voice broke on a sob and she shook her head bemusedly. She had a yearning to feel someone's arms around her, someone, her mind prayed, someone who would offer her comfort. He stood there watching her as

147

she sank into a chair. 'I cannot blame Jamie and I do not blame Ruari Beag,' she said quietly. 'He has always been kind enough to me. It is I who failed to make him happy.'

'You made him very happy,' he contradicted. 'Particularly when you accepted Jamie into this household. Not just accepted him but were keen to have him. I tell you no woman could have made him happier.'

She cupped her hands to her face to hide her tear-filled eyes.

'Will I go now and bring Jamie?' he asked her.

'Please,' she assented, and when Jamie came into the kitchen she held out her arms and hugged him to her, feeling his need for comfort. It was not until she was in bed that night that she called to mind that she had not offered Ruari Mhor a trace of commiseration over the loss of his brother.

Apart from the fact that they noticed Jamie's stammer seemed to have been cured, at least temporarily, by the tragedy they carried on stoically for the next few days, doing what needed to be done and doing nothing that was not necessary. Jamie accompanied Kirsty to the cattle. Ruari Mhor wandered about the shore. None of them seeming to know what they were expecting to happen until a few days later, Ruari Mhor came into the house and demanded Ruari Beag's seaboots.

Kirsty looked up at him, perplexed by the demand.

'They have found his body,' Ruari Mhor confirmed. His voice was harsh but she knew it was an attempt to disguise his grief.

'Why would you want his boots?' Kirsty asked nervously.

'He is to be buried tomorrow,' he replied. And when Kirsty still looked puzzled he went on, 'Do you not know the custom here?' She shook her head. 'When a man dies by accident in these parts his boots must always be buried beneath him.'

'What reason would there be for that?'

He looked at her gravely. 'It is so his ghost cannot walk,' he said.

She shuddered. 'I never heard of that,' she confessed and went to get her drowned husband's boots.

The sealed coffin was brought to the Island and placed on a bench outside the house. There was a mist rolling in from the sea and the land was eerily quiet. The male mourners, mostly recognisable as fishermen, grouped themselves loosely beside the bier as the missionary read the service. Mairi Jane stood close to Kirsty, offering support while the rest of the women stood around the doorway of the house.

When the service was over, the coffin was carried back to the boat and left, while the men there returned to sustain their genuine grief from a bottle while the women took sustenance from the teapot. After a while there came an urgent call for the mourners to get aboard the boat which had brought them and was now returning to the mainland, but since the bier was to be taken to a port nearer to the burial ground *The Two Ruaris* was to wait until the missionary was ready to go.

The missionary's wife waited with him. She was a thin stringy woman with a 'face like yesterday' as Mairi Jane described her, and a skin like faded calico. Even her smile was supercilious. Mairi Jane, who had volunteered to stay the night with Kirsty, made a grimace of disdain and disappeared but having cornered Kirsty, the couple sat in the kitchen taking more tea. Kirsty wished they would go but she supposed they thought they must stay to offer more comfort and condolence, and at the same time wring her soul with more prayers. But that was not why they had stayed, as she was soon to find out.

'What are you thinking of doing now?' the missionary's wife asked.

'Do? I've had little time for thinking,' Kirsty countered.

'Well, we think it best to tell you it wouldn't be right for you to stay on here, don't we, Lachlan?'

Kirsty fixed them with a puzzled glance.

'Stay in the same house with your husband's brother and no other woman to chaperone you! That will not fit in with church teaching,' she added relentlessly.

'Jamie Eilidh will be staying here for a time at least,' Kirsty told them.

'Your husband's sinfully begotten son,' the missionary's wife scorned. 'Surely that would not be condoned by the church, would it, Lachlan?' she appealed to her husband.

His mouth was full of scone and he answered with a barely perceptible nod.

'What do you suggest I do?' Kirsty demanded.

'Of course you must leave Westisle. The two of you would be disgraced by such a scandal,' she asserted. 'And your brother-in-law would not be welcome at Communion which he has always tried to attend when the weather allowed.'

Ruari Mhor came into the kitchen. 'The men are wanting away,' he announced. 'The tide is on the turn.'

The missionary and his wife shook hands with her, murmured an unintelligible blessing and followed him down to the boat.

Kirsty was resting her head on the table when Mairi Jane came into the kitchen. 'Indeed, what use are they to anyone?' she asked. 'He puts his stomach before his soul and she puts her fancies before facts.' She looked keenly at Kirsty. 'They've not been unkind to you, *mho ghaoil*?'

'No, no,' Kirsty denied. 'She just seems to think I'm much in need of her prayers – and not just because I've lost my man.'

'Ach, her!' Mairi Jane chortled her contempt.

When Ruari Mhor took Mairi Jane home next morning Kirsty went down to watch the boat crossing the Sound. The mist of the previous evening had cleared and, sitting on a knoll hugging her knees, she watched the boat receding. After it was out of sight she lifted her eyes to stare at the barren hills, their peaks black against the clear sky, putting her in mind of figures which had been suddenly petrified while leaping during an ecstatic dance.

A gull squawked as it swooped low. She felt acutely alone.

That night Kirsty found herself worrying about the missionary's wife's sharp assessment of her position. It seemed to her she was once again facing a vague and improbable future. The house, the whole of Westisle, undoubtedly belonged to Ruari Mhor. Her own Ruari had said that he and his brother had inherited it jointly from their parents, so what now? But it was not the legal aspect that troubled her, it was the moral aspect as preached by the missionary's wife. Ought she to live in the same house as her brother-in-law? Would Jamie be considered a suitable chaperone? Would Ruari Mhor blame her if he was excluded from Communion? But where could she go? She was certain, since he now knew she would soon be giving birth to his brother's child, that he would not send her away but she must not come between him and his church. She decided to put the position to him as soon as he came back from the burial ground, but when he did appear he looked so anguished, so beaten, she could only follow his movements with aching, compassionate eyes.

When she did speak to him about the missionary's wife's criticism of their living in the same house he said, 'You wish to go away?'

'No. I have nowhere to go.'

'Are you happy here?'

'I am. But just as I did not wish to come between you and your brother, neither do I wish to come between you and your church.'

'My faith is between myself and the Lord God. The missionary and his wife are outside it. But if you wish it I will offer to wed you.' She was so astounded she could only stare at him speechlessly. 'It would be a ceremony here at the house only. I would ask for nothing from you.'

Utterly flabbergasted she collapsed on to a chair. 'I hadn't thought of that as a possible solution,' she murmured.

'Very well, I will speak to the minister,' he said as he went out of the kitchen.

It was some minutes before she could get up from the chair.

'I had a feeling that this would happen,' said Jamie, when she told him.

'You had a feeling? How could you have a feeling about it? He has never welcomed me to this place. When I first came here he wouldn't speak to me for quite a while. Even now he prefers not to speak to me unless it's necessary. Certainly I have never had any feeling about him marrying me. I must tell you Jamie, I consented to this wedding only because I wanted a home.'

'But this is your home, surely?'

She told him of the missionary's wife's warnings, and that this was the way he had dealt with the problem.

'She told you that you couldn't continue to live here unless you married your husband's brother?' he asked incredulously.

'No, no. She certainly didn't suggest anything like that. She simply said I must leave Westisle. I daresay the idea of me marrying Ruari Mhor hadn't occurred to her any more than it had to me. It came like a bolt from the blue when he offered to marry me.'

'And this is my uncle's religion?' he queried scathingly. 'I will tell you now, I have no respect for a religion like that.'

She said, 'There are many different religions, Jamie, and we have to be tolerant when we speak of them. You yourself are of a religion that many folk despise.'

'I have no religion,' he said firmly.

'You were born of a strong Catholic family,' she pointed out.

'I am no longer a Catholic,' he said. 'I discovered a relationship with my Maker which no man shall despoil.

153

No priest, no nuns, no minister, no bishop nor archbishop.'

'Jamie!' She was shocked. 'You are young yet. You should not be so downright.'

'Ach, bugger the lot of them,' he almost spat.

'You haven't learned to use language like that in this house,' she reprimanded him.

He shrugged his shoulders. 'One learns to swear when one is at sea,' he said.

Her eyes followed him as he went across to the barn. He was no longer the lonely boy he had been before he came to Westisle. His stammer was hardly noticeable now. Fishing and landwork seemed to have broadened his shoulders. Westisle was helping him to grow into a fine sturdy lad, she thought.

'The minister will be across in a day or two,' Ruari Mhor told her one evening, and accepting that weather and tide would have to be taken into consideration she did not press for more precise information.

It was nearly a month later while she was busy about the house that Ruari Mhor and Jamie escorted the minister into the kitchen. Quickly she washed her hands and taking off her overall stood ready for the ceremony. Ruari Beag's ring was used for a second time. Afterwards the minister took a cup of tea and some buttered scones with them all, drank a glass or two of whisky and then with warm wishes he shook hands and announced he was ready to depart.

'I'm glad,' Jamie said to her when they were alone in the kitchen. He kissed her. 'It's good to know you'll always be here,' he said.

'It is to be only a semblance of a marriage,' she explained to him. 'Though it's my belief that folks will make a scandal of whatever they wish.' He nodded understandingly.

No mention was made of her pregnancy so she was surprised when Ruari Mhor came into the kitchen one day and asked unexpectedly, 'When is your bairn due?'

She was a little taken aback by the directness of his

question. 'Oh, any time now,' she told him. 'Mairi Jane will be willing to come over to Westisle to see me through the birth. She assures me she has had plenty of practice.'

He went to the door and looked out to sea. He called Jamie who was doing some weeding in Kirsty's vegetable garden and pointed out to him a large black dolphin-shaped cloud hovering in the pale grey of the sky. 'I am not liking the look of it,' he said. 'We had best go now and fetch Mairi Jane.'

'Not yet,' she called after them, but they were already out of earshot.

By the time Mairi Jane arrived the wind was already tearing at the clouds and by evening there was a full gale.

'My, my, but you did well to send for me when you did,' said Mairi Jane, divesting herself of her oilskin. 'This could blow for a week or more and I'm thinking you may not last that long.'

'I didn't send for you,' Kirsty was quick to tell her. 'It was Ruari Mhor himself who made up his mind to go for you. I couldn't stop him.'

'He is a wise man,' said Mairi Jane. 'He knows the sea and the sky and many another thing besides.'

Four days later when the gale was punching at the roof and lashing the sea to a white frenzy Kirsty's son was born. There were no complications and when Mairi Jane put the child into her arms Kirsty experienced an undreamed-of rapture. Oh, if only Ruari Beag could have known! If only he could have shared this moment with her. Tears filled her eyes as she chided herself for not having told him earlier. She had cheated him of the knowledge that she was to bear his child and a wave of depression swept over her as she recalled the inadequacy of her loving.

Mairi Jane came into the room bringing a tray of tea and scones. She sat on the bed and asked tenderly, 'What name is the bairn to have?'

'I suppose I shall call him Ruari after his father but for his second name I will call him Donny, after my Uncle

Donny who died when I was young. He was sent to a Home at the same time as I was sent to the city. He died at the Home and it has always troubled me that I was never able to say goodbye to him.'

Mairi Jane nodded. 'Ruari Mhor will welcome another Ruari and Donny is a nice enough name,' she approved.

Jamie was keen to greet his step-brother while Ruari Mhor, who had shown little interest in her confinement beyond making sure Mairi Jane was on hand to help, produced a beautiful cradle he had made from driftwood almost as soon as he'd heard the baby's first cry; and thereafter he had doted on the child as if it had been his own. When the bairn outgrew the cradle he constructed a cot and also a harness so that the child could be carried easily over the moors. He fenced a small area of grass which he kept well scythed so that when 'Wee Ruari' had reached the crawling and then the toddling stage there was no fear of him wandering too far away.

Kirsty experienced a feeling of tremendous fulfilment as she sat in the sun one day watching her bairn calling babyishly to Jamie and 'Yewyy' from his enclosure. They were a family, she told herself, even if two of its members were a little spurious.

When 'Wee Ruari' had progressed to a fairly sturdy toddler it was Ruari Mhor he insisted on following about and, glimpsing the big man coming home with the boy riding his broad shoulders, Kirsty would sometimes become aware of a strange surge of tenderness towards her dour brother-in-law. But she thought it was because of his obvious devotion to her child.

'He is growing fast,' observed Ruari Mhor one day. 'I am after thinking it will not be long before he will be needing to go to school.'

'Oh, not for a year or two yet,' Kirsty was quick to remind him. 'He is only past five years old just.'

'He's mighty eager to learn,' put in Jamie. 'When I was mending the creels the other day he wanted to try netting and I tell you he soon got the knack of it once I'd shown him how it was done. I believe his fingers are near as nimble as my own.'

'I believe he has the makings of a good scholar,' Ruari Mhor remarked, his tone disapproving Jamie's statement.

'I don't want to even think about him going to school yet,' Kirsty said.

'There are many things that need to be thought about,' Ruari Mhor reminded her, 'and time is for ever in a hurry. It will not wait.'

He spoke so solemnly that she flashed a curious glance at him, suspecting that his back might be troubling him again. But she dared not make mention of it.

Following upon the death of his brother, Ruari Mhor's zeal for fishing had flagged noticeably. It was to be expected, Kirsty thought. Not only had they been brothers but they had shared the close companionship of the sea. It would need the solace of time to mitigate his suffering.

Though he and Jamie had resumed lobster fishing it was not the compulsive occupation it had been in the past. Now it was Jamie who was the more eager to be off in the early mornings and as time went by it was becoming increasingly evident that it had become Jamie's task to see to the maintenance of the boat. Weather which Ruari Mhor would have disregarded when he was fishing with his brother now frequently made him question the wisdom of going to sea. Even the trips to the mainland to dispose of their catch and to take Kirsty's eggs, he sometimes murmured against disgruntledly.

Though, as Kirsty had hoped, the birth of her child had manifestly reanimated his spirits for a time and watching 'Wee Ruari' grow undoubtedly provided him with a good deal of pleasure, as the seasons passed it became plain that her brother-in-law was no longer the indefatigable man she had known. When the time for the outside work on the croft came round he tended to lean on his spade and let Jamie do most of the digging, saying jokingly that it was high time the boy learned to use

157

his strength, and though his manner towards herself still remained guarded he ceased to actually spurn her offers of help. She began to worry about him. After all, he was not an old man, she reminded herself. She voiced her concern to Jamie.

'Your uncle seems to be falling back in health again, Jamie. Do you think he is relapsing into grief over Ruari Beag's passing?'

'He is not the man he was,' Jamie conceded. 'I too am worried about him.'

'He wouldn't have had any mishap on board the boat, would he? I mean he hasn't strained himself hauling creels or anything like that?'

'Not to my knowledge,' said Jamie. 'But I reckon he is poorly. He stumbles a lot and he has dizzy fits sometimes when we're hauling.' He looked at her. 'A boat is no place for a dizzy man to be,' he added meaningfully.

'Would his back be troubling him again?' Jamie nodded gravely. 'Do you still walk his back for him?' she asked.

'As often as he asks me,' Jamie confirmed. 'And I hate to tell you how much bigger the lump is getting.'

'Lump!' echoed Kirsty agitatedly. 'I knew nothing of any lump. What do you suppose is causing that?'

'I don't know. He says it's nothing at all but I am sure it should not be there. I believe he is sometimes in great pain with it. He groans and moans during the night but when I ask him about it he says he was only snoring likely and that I must not speak to you of it.'

'What can we do, Jamie? He is so thrawn and will not hear of me getting a doctor, nor even a nurse to take a look at him.'

Jamie misinterpreting her question said, 'Myself will speak to Euan Ally about coming fishing with me. He's a good fisherman and not lacking in strength.'

'You don't think your uncle's illness is bad enough for that?' she asked despairingly.

Jamie did not spare her. 'I reckon the time is not all that far off when he will have to forsake the sea. I think he's beginning to know that for himself. If not, one of us must tell him.'

She looked at him aghast. 'Dear God!' she moaned. 'It will kill him to be told that. Who will tell him?'

'I think you should tell him,' said Jamie. 'You understand him.'

'Not I!' she caught her breath, momentarily shocked. 'I have never understood him, Jamie!' she declared.

Jamie regarded her sadly for a few moments before saying, 'If it will kill him to be told, it will, just as surely kill him not to be told,' he warned her. 'Together we must find a way to do it so that it will not wound him too much.' He paused. 'I am thinking I shall speak to Euan Ally about such things when next I see him.'

But it was Ruari Mhor himself who solved their dilemma.

A spell of wild weather followed their conversation, making fishing impossible. Kirsty was relieved since in such weather Ruari Mhor stayed in his bed for much of the day and though she knew he was ill the fact that he was in his bed was slightly less worrying for her than if he was out fishing. She was also relieved that she did not need to take hay to the cattle. When he was not at sea, Jamie always insisted on doing that and now they were a family of four they brought home two milking cows each night, separating them from their calves so she could easily milk them in the mornings.

Kirsty was busy making butter one day during the wild spell when Ruari Mhor came into the kitchen and sat in his chair beside the fire. 'Wee Ruari' immediately claimed his attention, anxiously offering him a mug of buttermilk. She'd seen her brother-in-law previously quaff a mug of buttermilk in one draught but today the hand holding the mug was trembling and he was drinking the milk slowly sip by sip. He looked across at her, and saw her watching him. With clumsy haste he attempted to put the mug down on the hob. There was a sizzle as some of the milk splashed on the fire.

'Wee Ruari' flinched away. 'Ach now, see you've filled the mug too full for Uncle Ruari,' Kirsty reproved him gently. 'Just because you like full mugs it doesn't mean everyone else does. You should have drunk some out of it first.'

'Ach, no, no indeed,' murmured Ruari Mhor consolingly. 'It is just that my hands have got so used to hauling in creels they treat everything else the same way.' He reached out an arm and pulled the child towards him. They smiled dotingly at each other.

A few minutes later they heard Jamie returning from the cattle and 'Wee Ruari' rushed out to meet him.

'The lad is gey fond of Jamie,' Ruari Mhor remarked.

'He is so,' agreed Kirsty. 'And Jamie is gey fond of "Wee Ruari". He has such patience with the boy. It does my heart good to see the care he takes of the child.'

'And it is likely he will take great care of you when the time comes,' he observed.

Jamie and 'Wee Ruari' came into the kitchen, 'Wee Ruari' proudly carrying a freshly shot rabbit.

'You took the gun?' Ruari Mhor looked at Jamie.

'Aye, I did. There's a deal of rabbits over by there. We could do with some guns from the mainland soon to take a few pots at them or we'll get over-run surely.' He shrugged out of his oilskin. 'They'll be keen enough to come I'm thinking.'

'I doubt they will,' agreed Ruari Mhor. 'Euan Ally was asking me last time he was out with us on the boat just if I'd be willing for him to have a day's shooting over here.'

Kirsty and Jamie exchanged a swift glance.

'You'd be willing for him to come?' Jamie asked his uncle eagerly. Ruari Mhor nodded. 'Will I tell him next time I see him?'

'You will tell him,' said Ruari Mhor. 'He is one that we can trust and he is wise enough.' His voice seemed to scratch the syllables and he spoke slowly as if his thoughts

160

were smudged by vagueness. But his meaning was clear enough.

Jamie went over and tapped the barometer. 'The glass is going up,' he reported. 'We should be back at sea soon enough. Maybe tomorrow.'

Kirsty, bending down to pick up the churn and take it through to the scullery, thought she caught an expression of anguish flit across her brother-in-law's face but he made no comment.

'I will take the churn for you,' Jamie offered. She followed him through to the scullery and when they returned to the kitchen Ruari Mhor was rising from his chair but seeing them he slumped back into it.

'When you speak to Euan Ally tell him there is likely a job going on the boat. Myself is thinking of taking a wee rest from the fishing for a whiley.' He tried a half-hearted chuckle. 'I feel hard of leaving my bed in the early mornings.'

Kirsty and Jamie exchanged panic-stricken glances. Could Ruari Mhor have overheard their discussion? Nevertheless his admission gave Kirsty her chance to plead: 'Ruari Mhor, you have a sickness and I am worried about you. You are having no medicine and I beg you to let me get you a doctor. You will not be able to go fishing until your strength is built up. Please, Ruari Mhor. You must not let illness take away your strength.'

His expression hardened. 'You will not speak to me again of calling a doctor.' His tone was reprimanding. 'If the Lord chooses He will give me back my strength.' Getting up from his chair he shuffled slowly out of the kitchen and as the door closed behind him she and Jamie stared at each other, helplessly shaking their heads.

'He is throwing his life away just,' Jamie croaked.

'I believe that's the way of it,' Kirsty moaned, covering her face with her hands. 'There is nothing we can do,' she murmured.

'I will bring Euan Ally across next time I see him,' Jamie said. 'I will tell him it is for a short time just but

I reckon he already is wise to what is happening to my Uncle Ruari. Many folks have been saying they don't like the look of him.' He went to the door and stood looking at the unsettled sky. When he came back into the kitchen he asked her, 'You will welcome Euan Ally?'

'As well as I can,' she said limply.

So Euan Ally came not only to fish but to share the work of the croft, while Ruari Mor seemed relieved to spend more and more of his time in his room, venturing out only when warm sunlight tempted him to seek the bench at the end of the house or when the smell of cooking wafting from the kitchen proved irresistible. But the time came when even these small ventures were beyond his strength and since he refused to allow her to take meals to him she had to rely on 'Wee Ruari's' services when Jamie was at sea.

'Why doesn't Uncle Ruari come into the kitchen any more and have his meals with us?' asked 'Wee Ruari'. 'He didn't ever want to stay in his bed like he does now.'

She said quickly, 'Uncle Ruari has a very sore leg and he has to rest it as much as he can.'

'Will he have to have his leg cut off like Padruig Bhann?'

'No, no. Nothing like that, I hope.' She spoke comfortingly although the child's innocent questions shook her.

'If he has his leg cut off Jamie is clever enough to make for him a wooden one, isn't he?'

She nodded assent and before she could prevent him he'd run off to his uncle's bedroom. She hoped he wouldn't ask him the same question.

A few minutes later he was back in the kitchen. 'Uncle Ruari wants you to do something for him,' he gabbled quickly as he ran outside to see how Jamie and Euan Ally were occupying themselves.

Kirsty was startled. 'Are you sure that was the message?' she called after him. She had to be content with an exaggerated nod flung at her as he raced after Jamie. She brewed a fresh pot of tea and as she timidly approached

Ruari Mhor's room she realised she would be entering her husband's bedroom for the first time. As she opened the door she saw that his bed was close beside the window and he had his back to the light. He looked momentarily surprised to see her and she wondered if he had already forgotten his message to her or if 'Wee Ruari' had interpreted it wrongly. She paused on the threshold.

' "Wee Ruari" said you wanted me to do something for you, so I have brought this mug of tea fresh from the pot,' she said lightly as she moved forward. She saw his brow was wet and he was wearing spectacles. There was an open Bible on the coverlet. 'I've never known you to wear spectacles,' she remarked.

'Only for reading the Good Book,' he replied. He tried to drink but the mug tilted in his weak grasp and much of the tea spilled over the bedclothes.

Gently she took the mug from him. 'I'll take your mug and refill it,' she told him as she mopped up the spill.

'No, no, there is still plenty left,' he insisted. 'Stay now since I have something to say to you which must be said before I make my journey.'

She thought for a second he must be wandering. 'What journey?' she asked blankly, but he ignored or did not hear her question.

'You must try to understand,' he began gravely. 'This Island of Westisle belonged jointly to Ruari Beag and myself. He willed his portion to yourself and Jamie, and I have willed my portion to yourself also and to your own "Wee Ruari". When the Lord sees fit to change me, everything I possess will be yours and your son's to have. You will not want.'

'I wish to take nothing from you,' she said. 'I am content with what I have. And I will not let you talk of being changed. You are still a young man and if you would let me call a doctor he would get you into the hospital and we would see you cured again in no time. Please, Ruari Mhor. Please,' she pleaded desperately.

'No!' he almost shouted. 'I have not long. I have prayed

163

to the Lord and He will have mercy and not allow me to suffer this pain for many hours longer.' She looked at him horrified.

'No, no,' she cried. 'Please let me call a doctor.' She sought for his limp hands and held them firmly in hers.

'A doctor would tell you it is too late.' He was breathing with difficulty. Her eyes filled with tears. 'Now, I want you to go to that drawer and open it,' he said.

Obediently she went across to a large chest of drawers. 'This one?' she asked, her hand resting on the knob of the top drawer.

'That one,' he affirmed. 'There is a wee carved box in there. Bring it over to me.' She did what he asked. 'Open it,' he bade her. She opened it and then handed the box to him. 'See this now,' he said, while his fumbling fingers removed a piece of cloth from inside the box to reveal a large brooch. 'This was given to my mother by the old Laird's wife and my mother gave it to me to give to my wife when I married. I never did marry. Not rightly,' his eyes appealed for her understanding, 'so, the brooch has stayed in the box. Now I want you to have it.' He held it out to her with a shaky hand.

'For me?' she exclaimed incredulously.

He reached out to touch the hand with which she was holding the brooch and for a moment she thought he was reaching to take it away from her.

'No, no,' he said irritably as she tried to give it back to him. 'I was not kind to you when my brother first brought you here.'

'You were never unkind,' she corrected him.

'It was wrong of me. You were a good wife to Ruari Beag and you are a near mother to Jamie.' Again he paused for breath. 'Now I want you to have this and keep it in memory of my brother and of myself.'

'I need nothing like this to keep the memory of either of you alive,' she said. Half-blinded by tears she wiped the back of her hand across her eyes and studied the brooch. 'It is a beautiful brooch,' she enthused, 'and much too grand a thing for me to wear.'

He held out his empty tea mug. 'Get me another mug of tea,' he directed her, trying to inject a tone of brusqueness into his voice.

When she returned to the room with another mug of tea he was lying back on his pillows. He said, 'Your son will be a credit to Ruari Beag. I could wish that I too had a son from you but you belonged to my brother.' She was staring at him with widening eyes. 'You mind the day my brother brought you here and the wind blew off your bonnet?' She nodded briefly. 'That day I tell you your hair wound itself around my heart and so it has been since. Even today the glow of it warmed and brightened this room when you came into it. But you were my brother's woman and I had to steel my heart against you.' Kirsty was shaking her head in confused disbelief as she listened to him and suddenly comprehension flashed into her mind. She recalled how she'd yearned for someone's arms to be around her when he'd told her of Ruari Beag's death. And she knew now for whose arms she had yearned. In her mind's eye she could see him clearly, standing in the doorway; just as clearly she could hear the stark message he had for her, 'the sea has claimed him'. And it had been because she dared not seek his arms that she had fainted.

Her knees weakened and she collapsed beside the bed. 'Ruari!' she whispered brokenly. 'Ruari, *mho gradh, a chiali mo chridhe*,' she cried, desperately grasping his hands and covering them with kisses. Through her tears she met his questioning eyes. 'Ruari, don't leave me. I need you. I need you.' His eyes caressed her. His grim mouth softened and he reached to stroke her hair. She kissed his forehead, his cheeks and then pressed her lips to his mouth but he made no attempt to reciprocate. 'I must not betray my brother,' he said, and again his eyes were pleading for understanding.

He lay back on the pillow, holding his spectacles.

'Kirsty,' he said, 'I have always been able to read the Good Book but today I cannot do that. My spectacles seem to be dirty.' He held them out to her and though they looked to be clear enough she polished them on the inside of her apron and helped him put them on his nose. Shakily he tried to pick up the Bible. 'No, it's no better,' he complained. 'It must be the window that is dirty. You will give the glass a rub.'

Jamie had cleaned the windows the previous evening and their clarity was plain enough. All the same she reached over the bed and made a pretence of polishing the glass.

'There now, is that better?'

She held the Bible close to his eyes but they were slowly closing. He managed to say, 'You never were any good at cleaning windows.' His head fell back on the pillow and in the long moment that followed she knew that the only man she had ever loved was gone from her.

OTHER ARROW BOOKS

☐ The Hills is Lonely	Lillian Beckwith	£3.99
☐ Sea For Breakfast	Lillian Beckwith	£2.99
☐ Hebridean Omnibus	Lillian Beckwith	£7.99
☐ The Small Party	Lillian Beckwith	£2.99
☐ Second Hebridean Omnibus	Lillian Beckwith	£7.99
☐ Bruach Blend	Lillian Beckwith	£3.99
☐ Dublin 4	Maeve Binchy	£3.99
☐ The Lilac Bus	Maeve Binchy	£3.99
☐ Frenchman's Creek	Daphne Du Maurier	£4.99
☐ Jamaica Inn	Daphne Du Maurier	£4.99
☐ My Cousin Rachel	Daphne Du Maurier	£4.99
☐ Rebecca	Daphne Du Maurier	£4.99
☐ King Hereafter	Dorothy Dunnett	£4.99
☐ Damage	Josephine Hart	£5.99
☐ Black Sheep	Georgette Heyer	£3.99
☐ Frederica	Georgette Heyer	£4.99
☐ Lady of Quality	Georgette Heyer	£3.99
☐ First Man in Rome	Colleen McCullough	£6.99
☐ Sleeping with the Enemy	Nancy Price	£4.99
☐ Oriental Hotel	Janet Tanner	£4.99

ARROW BOOKS, BOOKSERVICE BY POST, PO BOX 29, DOUGLAS, ISLE OF MAN, BRITISH ISLES

NAME————————————————————

ADDRESS————————————————————

————————————————————————

————————————————————————

Please enclose a cheque or postal order made out to Arrow Books Ltd. for the amount due and allow the following for postage and packing.

U.K. CUSTOMERS: Please allow 30p per book to a maximum of £3.00

B.F.P.O. & EIRE: Please allow 30p per book to a maximum of £3.00

OVERSEAS CUSTOMERS: Please allow 35p per book.

Whilst every effort is made to keep prices low it is sometimes necessary to increase cover prices at short notice. Arrow Books reserve the right to show new retail prices on covers which may differ from those previously advertised in the text or elsewhere.